No.8 The

Kerran Daly

In support of West Norfolk Deaf Association

No.8 The Old Bookshop

ABIGAIL STORM
AND THE
MOUNTAIN OF DREAMS

Kerran Daly

All characters in this novel are fictitious and any resemblance to real persons, living or dead, is purely coincidental

Copyright © Kerran Daly 2022

The right of Kerran Daly to be identified as the author of the work has been asserted to him in accordance with the Copyright, Designs and Patents Act 1988.

All rights reserved. No part of this publication may be reproduced, stored in a retrieval system, or transmitted, in any form or by any means without the prior written permission of the publisher, nor otherwise circulated in any form of binding or cover other than that in which it is published and without a similar condition being imposed on the subsequent publisher

ISBN 978-1-915787-10-1

Printed by Biddles Book Printers

www.Biddles.co.uk, Blackborough End, Kings Lynn, Norfolk

Special thanks to:

Sarah Cox – Front cover artwork -
'No. 8 The Old Bookshop' ©

Shona Hughes-Daly – Back Cover artwork –
'Downham Market Clock Tower' ©

Shona Hughes-Daly - Cover design ©

Song 'My Netherland' by kind permission of

Nico Dobben - Bandcamp ©

Carole and Shona for first draft reading and constructive feedback.

All staff and volunteers at

No.8 The Old Bookshop, Downham Market.

~ CHAPTER ONE ~

Snowfall on Bexwell

It was the first day of the New Year and the little Norfolk town of Downham Market lay under a fresh blanket of snow. It was the first snow of the winter and up on Bexwell Road, the Storm family had finished their lunchtime meal. The children had stacked the dishes in the dishwasher and were now getting ready to go down to the Howdale to meet friends and have a bit of fun in the snow.

Despite the fact they were aged fourteen, twelve and ten, their mother, in her typical busy manner, fussed around them checking they all had their boots, coats, hats and gloves whilst telling Abigail, the eldest, to be sure they were all back by four o'clock before it got too dark, well in time for tea.

'Yes, yes,' said Abi. Like most teenagers of her age she felt she was almost an adult and wished her mum wouldn't go on so much.

'We're only going down the road Mum. I mean it's only Downham.' Her tone implied that nothing ever happened in Downham and as far as she could recall, so far, nothing ever had.

Zach, the middle one of the three, pulled on his Norwich City bobble hat and tucked his long, curly locks in underneath as a token gesture towards looking tidy. He knew that if he didn't do it himself his mother would do it for him and he cringed at the thought. Unfortunately for Zach, as her only boy, she doted on him even more than she did on her youngest, Izzie.

Izzie looked very much like a smaller version of Abi. She had the same shoulder-length, jet black, straight hair. They both had an identical fringe that sat just above the eye-line and gave them a sort of secretive look. Izzie didn't mind how much or how little her mother fussed over her, she was far too dreamy to notice.

Mr Storm was parked by the fire with the television on, complaining as usual about the lack of television worth watching. Abi clipped on their rusty-coloured Border terrier Millie's lead and they headed off. Five minutes or so later they reached the park. It was pretty crowded with children of all ages and sizes. Some they knew, some they didn't. Some they knew but wished they didn't. Bucko Braithwaite for instance.

Bucko was in Zach's class at Downham Academy

and Bucko was trouble. Zach knew he had to stay on the right side of him. Everyone knew it would be best if they stayed on the right side of Bucko. At the same time, you didn't want to get too close and end up as one of his sidekicks. It was a tricky balancing act but Zach consoled himself with the thought that these early lessons in dealing with trouble would help prepare him for making his way in the world, later on in life. Zach liked to justify his actions in a positive way, no matter what the real reasons for them were.

Abi hurriedly tied up Millie's lead to a handy, metal railing and told her to 'Stay'. Then they were off, talking to their friends and generally hanging out having a laugh. Zach helped Izzie build a snowman. Much of the time making it was spent chasing each other around with great lumps of snow, often ending up side by side, flat on their backs, laughing heartily as their cheeks reddened

Abi was regularly checking on Millie to make sure she was okay and every half hour or so she went over, untied her and walked her around on her lead so that she could move about and keep warm. On the fourth or fifth time she was walking Millie, Abi wandered over to where Zach and Izzie were resting a little to get their breath back.

'We've got some time before we need to be back,' she said. 'Millie could do with a bit more of a walk. I'm thinking of going down to the town centre to see what's going on and then along the High Street and back up Bexwell that way. You both happy to come?'

Neither Zach nor Izzie wanted to go straight home so they agreed and they set off. It wasn't long before they were telling Millie to 'sit' at Church Road so she was ready to cross over on their say so. Once across, they took the few short steps down Rampant Horse Lane and finally turned right into the High Street.

The Christmas lights were still up, giving the centre of town a warm festive glow. The streets were quiet with not many people about. Zach glanced up at the beautifully ornate town clock and noticed it was just on quarter to four. Forgetting for a moment that everything would be closed, it being New Year's Day, the three of them automatically made a beeline for their favourite shop in town, 'No.8 The Old Bookshop', just along the High Street on the left.

This lovely little bookshop had been very much a part of their lives since they were toddlers and is still somewhere they regularly enjoy visiting. Each in turn had gone up the Yellow Brick Road with Dorothy, down the rabbit hole with Alice and all the way to Neverland with Peter Pan. Their dad especially likes going with them, offering advice on books he had enjoyed when he was their age. Apart from that it gives him the opportunity to search the music section in pursuit of obscure titles on jazz and skiffle.

While he happily buys them books from the shop for their Christmas or birthdays, he insists that at other times they should pay half the cost out of their pocket money. He does this to teach them the value of money, a gift he believes it is important to instill in his children so that they appreciate what they have. This tactic seems to be paying off. They are happy to spend part of their pocket money on books rather than all of it on sweets. When they don't have enough for both, choices have to be made.

A good number of the books they buy are filled with enchanting tales of wonder, mystery, fantasy and adventure. They're often set in exotic, far-off lands and help open their minds up to new and fascinating places and ideas that bring happiness and solace to each of them in equal measure. Others are silly and funny and just as enjoyable.

Being a secondhand, charity bookshop it is more affordable and more intriguing than the average bookshop. The sort of shop both adults and children love poking around in, never knowing what little gem they might find lurking, waiting to be discovered by someone new, for the umpteenth time. A shop with a hint of the magical about it, mixed with more than a little of the warmth and comfort of bygone days.

Characters from the books can often be found making unexpected appearances, anywhere at any time. You just never know when they might pop up. They could be peeking out from behind a vase of flowers on the top shelf or hanging from the ceiling in a hot air balloon, giving a friendly wave. You might find yourself sitting next to Winnie The Pooh or Harry Potter's Sorting Hat perched on one of the chairs, where you are invited to rest and browse through literary gems on every subject under the sun.

Apart from the cost aspect, the children, have other reasons for buying their books from No.8. Being secondhand, they never know what oddities they might find hidden inside them. Budding artists and critics from preceding generations sometimes left pearls of wisdom for the future reading public. Everything from witty side comments in the margins, to pencil drawings of their favourite characters. Paddington bear seems to be a popular choice for the young doodlers of Norfolk.

Dedications are another source of interest. On one occasion Abi came across an Agatha Christie in which someone had written 'To Angie, guess who?' Beside it they had put a solitary, inky fingerprint. This had been followed by a series of other fingerprints dotted around, presumably left by its various new owners. Beside one of these, someone had sketched Sherlock Holmes carefully studying it with his magnifying glass. Underneath, someone else had written 'Sherlock is Sir Arthur Conan Doyle not Agatha Christie. Twit.'

As they stood outside, Abi bent down to pull her socks up inside her boots and handed Millie's lead to Izzie. Izzie was staring in through the window at one of the wonderful shop displays which were much admired for their imaginative impact and never ceased to delight passers-by. She was leaning up close and gazing, in her wide-eyed, dreamy way. The display was a wintry Christmas scene out on the fen. Tiny people in hats, gloves and scarves were skating on the frozen waters as geese flew overhead in V formation.

As she stared and stared, her gaze took her further into the shop where something gave cause for her to peer even harder. She wrinkled her eyes up tight and squinted into the very back where she thought she could see something moving. Then, she could just make out a rather scary looking lady in a long black cloak wearing a crown, who seemed to be giving instruction to a very tall gentleman with dark glasses and a white stick. Izzie kept staring and staring, deeper and deeper into the shop trying to make out what they were doing till everything became a bit of a blur …

#

~ CHAPTER TWO ~

The Clock Tower

Abi was running just as fast as she could down the High Street chasing after Millie. Zach was running after her, followed by Izzie. They were all running and shouting as loud as they could.

'Stop! Millie, stop!'

Millie was dashing towards the clock tower at full speed with her lead trailing behind her.

As Abi got closer she could see that the small maintenance panel door at the back of the clock was open. She had just about reached Millie and was bending down about to grab her, when Millie wriggled through the open door and disappeared inside. Abi pulled the door a little more open and ducked down and went in after her, closely followed by Zach. Izzie got there a few seconds later and as soon as she was inside, the panel door closed behind her.

'Oh Izzie, you idiot,' cried Abi. 'Why did you shut the door? Can't you see there's no handle on the inside? We won't be able to get out again.'

'I didn't shut it, I swear I didn't, it just closed on its own behind me, honest Abi, honest,' said Izzie as she turned around and pushed at the door, but it wouldn't budge. All three of them then stood staring at the inner workings of the clock. The lights that kept it illuminated at night gave off a soft, warm glow as its flywheels, pulleys and chains and all sorts of working parts endlessly ticked and clunked away.

'Where's Millie gone?' said Izzie.

With their eyes more accustomed to the light, they all looked around for her and in the very back corner Abi spotted an open hatchway with a flight of stairs leading down underground.

'There,' she said pointing towards them. 'She must have gone down there.' They edged closer and peered into the depths. There were at least thirty steps going down and they could make out a row of dim lights with some sort of solid platform at the bottom.

'Nothing for it. There's no way back. Come on,' said Abi as she started on her way down.

As they neared the bottom they became aware of the familiar pattering of Millie's paws. All of a sudden she rushed up the last few steps full of excitement, jumping around wildly and wagging her tail.

Once she had settled down they walked the few paces out onto the edge of the platform. It was clear they were in some sort of tunnel with a river or a canal stretching off into the distance. A small, blue rowing boat sat at the edge of the platform, rocking gently in the relatively calm waters. Strangely, although it wasn't tied up in any way, it just sat there as if it was waiting for them. Abi and Zach gave knowing looks conveying to each other their anxiety at the weirdness of it all. So as not to worry Izzie, they both put a brave face on it. Abi, being Abi, then took control.

'Come on Izzie, we'll soon be home,' she said as she stepped into the boat and put out her hand to help Izzie aboard. Zach got in behind them and, moments later, they were rowing down the river with Abi at the oars, heading for a speck of light in the distance.

~ CHAPTER THREE ~

The Cauldron

Zach sat with his arm around Izzie's shoulder and his other hand firmly grasping Millie's collar. Abi was striking out with the oars in confident, measured strokes as if she had done it all her life. In reality she had only had one lesson from her mother, but then Abi is Abi.

Less than five minutes later they had reached the end of the tunnel. As they came out into the light, they found themselves in a beautiful sunlit pool with sheer rock faces on either side. There were great cascades of sparkling water pouring over them, thundering down into the depths below.

Abi rested the oars and they sat silently as they stared in awe and amazement. The rocky faces were enormously high. On top of them, great trees reached even further skyward and huge, brightly-coloured birds were perched in their branches. Others flew in wide circles, higher still above the treetops, cawing loudly in a deep blue, cloudless sky.

'Where do you think we are?' Zach asked, not really expecting either of them to answer.

'It's beautiful, like in a dream,' Izzie replied in a small, quiet voice full of wonder and delight. Millie climbed over and nuzzled up next to her panting heavily with her tongue hanging out. They both sat there, side by side, staring wide-eyed.

The sight of the pair of them happily gawping in sheer wonder at the dramatic landscape that now surrounded them caused Zach to give Abi another small sideways glance of surprise at Izzie's seemingly unworried reaction to what was happening. Not wanting to change that, and feeling it was his turn to give Izzie some reassurance that all was well and there was no need to worry, he prepared himself to speak in as normal a voice as possible.

'Well, wherever we are, we haven't come far, so like Abi says I'm sure we'll be home soon.'

'No,' said Izzie quietly under her breath, still staring straight ahead. 'We have come a long way, a very, very long way indeed.'

Where the waterfalls poured down either side, they did so from such a height that they formed a thick layer of dense spray between them. Abi picked up the oars and headed straight for it. They were soon lost in the middle of the misty tumult which formed a narrow channel between the roaring torrents on either side. Abi kept right on, steering the boat by the sound of the water crashing down around them. After no more than a minute or two, though it seemed much longer, they suddenly emerged out into the calm waters of the fen. The fen looks much the same whatever part of it you are in and there was nothing familiar to give them a clue as to exactly where they might be.

The air was warm and comforting compared to the snows they had left behind. Abi rested the oars again and took her hat, scarf and coat off. She then helped Izzie with hers and put them in the bottom of the boat. Zach did the same and as he took his bobble hat off, his golden locks fell down and danced around his cheeks. He wiped an arm across his brow and took a deep breath of the fresh, warm, wholesome air.

'What's that clippity cloppity noise?' said Izzie.

'What clippity cloppity noise? I can't hear anything,' replied Abi. With that, Millie's ears shot up as the gentle sound of a tuneful lute and a man's voice singing sweetly, came floating over from the right-hand bank:

'As I rode in to Downham town

Upon St Winnold's Day

The sweetest maid that ere I saw

Came walking down my way'

They all three spun round as one to see a young man astride a beautiful chestnut horse, lute in hand. He seemed just as surprised to see them as they were to see him. He immediately stopped singing and, with a bow of his head and a sweep of his feathered cap, addressed them with a beaming smile.

'Good day young ladies and good day to you too young sir. What brings you here on this fine morn?'

He had only just got the words out of his mouth when Abi came straight back at him.

'Good morning to you, sir. Surely it is only proper for you to introduce yourself and tell us about your business before asking about ours?' she said, in her usual confident and forthright manner.

'Will o' Castle Acre at your service ma'am and to tell you the truth I am doing what I always do, I am searching. I'm a fine, young fellow on a horse and every fine, young fellow on a horse is searching for something. If he had nothing to search for, what would he do and what would he have to sing mournfully about? A dog may lose his bone, a king may lose his crown and a young man on a horse may lose his sweet maid. Such is the way of the world and ever shall it be so.'

'And have you lost your sweet maid, sir?' asked Abi.

'Yes indeed for I cannot find her and if I cannot find her, she must be lost. Her name is Polly. She has red ribbons in her hair and is the prettiest maid in all the world.'

'You lost her sir?' said Abi, this time in a rather more hesitant voice. 'That was rather careless of you was it not?'

'No, no young lady, indeed I took great care but sometimes, despite the fact that five and five make ten and the world is round, sometimes no matter how careful you are, you can still lose things very dear to you. I would caution you, take heed. So, now you know who I am and what I am doing, can I ask again, what brings you here on this fine morn?'

The last thing Abi wanted to do at this point was to possibly upset Izzie by saying that they were lost and searching for their way home, so instead she patted Millie on the head and said they were taking their dog for a walk. Zach smiled a quiet smile of admiration for the way the young gentleman accepted with good grace, that taking a dog for a walk in a boat was the most natural thing in the world.

'Ah, and a very fine dog it is too,' he replied. 'I see you have no Guide so may I ask, who brought you through the Cauldron?' Zach felt that he had been silent long enough.

'The Cauldron sir? What is the Cauldron?'

'Why, the raging waterfalls that guard the entrance. Who brought you through them?'

'Well, Abi brought us through them. She rowed a straight path and here we are.'

'You came through the Cauldron on your own without the Guide? Utterly remarkable young lady, I have never heard the like.'

Then, looking around at the fen that looked much like any other part of the fen, Zach asked him if he knew by any chance just exactly where they were.

'Did the Herald not explain it all to you?'

'The Herald, what Herald?'

'What, no Guide and no Herald to welcome you and announce your arrival?' It was clear that the young man found this most unusual.

'How very odd.' he muttered to himself. 'How very odd indeed. Please forgive me but I must be on my way and return to my search. Without Polly I am only half the man I was, and half a man is as much use as a fiddle without a bow.'

With that he smiled politely, took hold of the reins and, with a great flourish, bowed and bid them adieu. His horse turned its head to look at the three of them rather disdainfully, snorted a little and then they trotted off into the distance. All three, along with Millie, sat in silence watching them spellbound as they disappeared out of sight.

~ CHAPTER FOUR ~

The Guardian

Zach asked Abi if she would like him to row for a while. She just gave him a withering look, clearly indicating that would simply hinder their progress and then pulled even harder on the oars. Seconds later she peered up at him from under her jet black fringe with a smile that said sorry, I love you really. Zach smiled back with brotherly understanding.

Zach was the sort of boy who could never be angry with either Abi or Izzie for very long. They teased him terribly, which only made Zach feel even more accepted and loved by both of them. Occasionally they would annoy him, but he just couldn't stay mad at them for more than a minute or two.

As she rowed on, he sat there with his arm around

Izzie's shoulder watching Abi row with steady, perfectly timed strokes. He was thinking how much he admired her positive attitude in her pursuit of excellence in everything she set out to do. With their father being a teacher and their mother a fitness instructor, she had been honed into the peak of physical and mental condition, but she never let that go to her head. Just as he was thinking about how she had never let him down, he suddenly recalled the only time she had, the Snape Lane incident.

It was back in the days when he was around four years old and Abi was about six or so. They had been visiting Granny Moffat in her little cottage at the top end of Bennet Street. Her cottage, like many of the houses in Downham, was made out of the local gingerbread stone and being surrounded by trees, it always reminded the children of the Hansel and Gretel story. Nanny Moffat, who was quite tall and lean with a long nose, used to hug them all a little too tightly.

Despite that, Zach loved going to nanny Moffat's. This was chiefly because she was quite liberal with the treat jar no matter how disapprovingly their mother looked at her. Also, she had a large, brightly-coloured parrot, that the late grampy Moffat had taught to say such phrases as 'Flippin' 'eck', 'Give's a ciggy,' and 'Put that light out,' as well as Zach's favourite, 'On The Ball City,' which was Norwich City's most famous chant back in the day.

When they were suitably rested and fed, watered

and toileted, they would say their goodbyes and walk back up towards the town using Snape Lane. At the top they turned right passing the old schoolmaster's house and the old school, then left up Paradise Road, round into Cannon Square, up Bexwell Road and home.

He remembered how on this particular visit to Granny Moffat's, when they were in the garden together, Abi had told him a ghostly tale about Old Rollie and Snape Lane. She put on her best spooky voice and told him that back in the time of the St Winnold's Day horse fair, one wet, windy and stormy night, a large, fiery black stallion broke loose from its stable and bolted down Snape Lane, spouting fire from its nostrils as it charged onwards at full gallop. Old Rollie the boatman was making his way up the lane, lantern in hand, on his way home, when the stallion hurtled into him, smashing him to the ground and trampling him to death.

'So,' she had said to him, 'if you go to Snape Lane on the night of St Winnold's day and the weather is stormy and wet, you will see the shadowy figure of Old Rollie with his lantern, swinging its way up the lane. Then you'll hear the thunder of hooves, the loud neighing of the horse and Old Rollie's horrible piercing cry as he meets his gruesome and bloody end.'

For about a year or so after that Zach was pleased to see the back of Snape Lane and his parents were a little curious as to why he always held their hand as they went up it. It had taken a little longer than usual for him to forgive her.

She had rowed on for about twenty minutes or so when they came across an elderly looking man with a white beard who was dressed in a naval Captain's uniform. He wore an eyepatch over his left eye and a naval cap with a band round it which, instead of it reading 'Captain', or 'Chief Petty Officer' or whatever, it read, 'Guardian'. He was sat on a folding, canvas chair next to some moorings. To one side of his chair stood a loudhailer and a briefcase. On the other side there was a V board with a notice on it, which simply read:

ALL VISITORS <u>MUST</u> SIGN IN

AT

THE CASTLE

Abi eyed him with suspicion as she thought that he looked too much like a naval captain to actually be a naval captain. As they drew up level with him he leaned over and grabbed his loudhailer.

'Do you have anything to declare?' he shouted in as loud and clear a voice as he could muster.

All three of them looked at each other with a touch of bewilderment. It was plain that the loudhailer was either a fake or it was broken, as it failed to make his voice any louder. Even Millie looked at him with her head on one side as if she was trying to understand what the funny shaped object was for.

'What sort of thing?' said Abi, unable to imagine what you might have to declare to visit a castle.

'What sort of thing? What sort of thing? The sort of things that are on the prohibited list of course,' the Guardian replied through the silent loudhailer, in a voice filled with exasperation.

'What prohibited list?' continued Abi.

'The prohibited list the Herald gave you,' said the Guardian in a long, drawn out, weary sort of tone designed to indicate that he had heard it all before.

'Sorry but we haven't met the Herald, so we don't have the list but, if you could show us the list we could check and let you know if we have anything to declare,' said Abi in a matter-of-fact sort of way.

'What do you mean, you haven't met the Herald. Didn't the Guide introduce you to him?' said the Guardian.

'No, we haven't met the Guide either,' explained Abi.

The Guardian was by this time clearly disturbed that procedures had not been correctly followed. Never before had anyone arrived saying they had not met the Guide or the Herald and not read the list. He gave a weary sigh of frustration and leaned over and made a great fuss of opening his briefcase. He then took out a long scroll which he held out and let fall all the way down to just above the water.

The three of them stared at it with some more

bewilderment and a good amount of amusement that they did their best to stifle. It read:

Summoner's list of items which MUST be declared

- Malicious intent -

- Concealed weapons -

- Snorkeling gear -

- Poetry of any description -

- Dietary requirements -

- Green socks -

- A lack of social skills -

- Motion sickness -

- Murder mystery fiction –

It was clear to Abi that the question 'do you have any of these items to declare?' would inevitably result in tedious, long debates about such things as how bad would your social skills need to be to correctly declare that you lacked social skills, and could malicious intent or concealed weapons still be malicious and concealed if you declared them? To avoid such drawn-out, time-consuming arguments, she decided on everyone's behalf, just to say that they didn't have anything to declare.

'What about batrachophobia?' said the Guardian as he rolled up the scroll, put it back in the briefcase and then turned towards them with a beaming inquisitive smile on his face. Zach was pretty certain that he could safely reply on behalf of all three of them.

'Batrachophobia? No, we can't declare that because it's not on the list and I am perfectly sure that if it were, we wouldn't know what it was anyway.'

'Well swing me from the yardarm. Rowing these waters not knowing whether you have batrachophobia. Why, that is one of the most dangerous things you can have out on the fen. Batrachophobia is the fear of toads, frogs and all amphibians. What if you didn't know you had batrachophobia and suddenly came across a newt face to face, imagine the carnage that might cause.'

Again all three of them looked at each other suitably mystified. Abi then took it on herself to state, once again in a matter-of-fact manner, they still had nothing to declare.

'Good,' said the Guardian. 'That'll save me a lot of time and paperwork. I hate paperwork. Paper really doesn't go well with this watery environment. Tie up at the moorings and follow the signs.'

'Thank you very much,' said Izzie just because she hadn't spoken for a while and being polite, she thought she ought to say something.

'You are very welcome young miss,' the Guardian replied. 'Just doing my job.'

They were glad to get the Guardian's approval and to start heading towards the castle, mainly because they were getting quite peckish and thought they might stop there for a little while and have something to eat, that being generally what they did when they visited castles.

Abi heaved to, and they tied up at the moorings. Having no need for their coats and winter wear they left them in the boat, all except Zach's bobble hat which he stuck in his pocket for safekeeping.

His 'Canaries' bobble hat was a tenth birthday present and his prize possession. It was the standard green and yellow of Norwich City with a ring of yellow canaries in a circle around the green, lower turned up rim. Despite it being the standard Norwich City bobble hat, many a fan had admired it for its 'Fly Canaries Fly' slogan his mother had embroidered on it for him.

As he put it in his pocket, Zach became a little homesick. It reminded him of the time his dad had tried to explain to him why they were called the Canaries. All he could remember was that it had something to do with cloth workers coming over from Flanders to Norwich and bringing their canaries with them. Despite the fact that his dad was a teacher by profession, his attempt to explain this to him during a crucial promotion game with the score at 1:1 with only ten minutes to go and Norwich only needing a draw, was not surprisingly largely unsuccessful. Bobble hat safely stowed away they started off.

On their first sighting of the castle they were, to say

the least, a little disappointed. It seemed quite a small castle, as castles go, only a tiny bit higher than the one or two houses that stood around it.

Izzie seemed unconcerned with the situation and not half as perturbed as Abi and Zach thought she might be, considering how strange everything was. To be fair though, they had always known she was more than a little mysterious.

On one occasion, a classmate of Abi's, Lucy Barnes, approached her to let her know that Izzie had been acting weirdly in the playground.

'Why? What did she do?' asked Abi.

'Well,' said Lucy. 'She was stood on her own in the middle of the playground singing quietly to herself with her arms pointing up to the heavens, when Jinky Jenkins, the P.E. teacher, asked her what she was doing. She said she was singing to the moon. When Miss Jenkins asked her why she was singing to the moon, Izzie said it was because she thought it would be a little sad and lonely spinning round and round in space all on its own. I thought I should let you know as she looked a little pale and I wondered if she was okay?'

Abi, who didn't think that was anything like unusual behaviour for Izzie, politely thanked Lucy for her concern and left it at that.

As they led the way, Izzie walked Millie along on her lead a little way behind them and sang quietly to herself. That was something she did a lot. It was a little song neither Abi, nor Zach had ever heard before:

'When you go walking in the fen
All on a summer's day
The moorhen and the crazy coot
Will cheer you on your way'

'The noble swan and the crested grebe
Will bow as you pass by
The ducks all laugh and chatter
As 'Good day to you,' they cry'

'But mind your step and have a care
Be careful how you go
For all is not quite as it seems
Out in the lowlands low'

'Out in the lowlands low,
Oh out in the lowlands low
All is not quite as it seems
Out in the lowlands low'

'When the light shines on the waters

Every now and then

Horizons sometimes slip away

And then drift back again'

'And when the sun is sinking down

Out upon the fen

Keep one eye out for Old Black Shuck

And one for the Lantern Men'

'So mind your step and have a care

Be careful how you go

For all is not quite as it seems

Out in the lowlands low'

The castle driveway was a good half a mile long and there were rhinoceroses along with the cows and sheep grazing the fields either side. Off to the right there was also a large pond with hippopotamuses wallowing in the mud while flocks of geese, ducks and flamingos mingled in and around them. Despite the strangeness of it all,

Izzie and indeed Millie, didn't seem to notice so Abi and Zach carried on as if nothing unusual was afoot. As they got closer, it was Abi who first mentioned that the castle seemed to be getting bigger by the minute.

'Well,' said Zach. 'It's perfectly normal for things to get bigger as you get closer to them.'

'Yes Zach, but now it's twice as high as the buildings surrounding it and growing even higher with every step.' Zach had to admit that that wasn't perfectly normal.

By the time they reached it, the castle was at least five storeys high. It was topped by a large, blue and gold flag which had on it a scary looking lady with an evil grin on her face. She was wearing a black cloak and had a gold crown on her head. She was flanked on either side by two huge sea monsters with barbed, harpoon-shaped tails and serpent-like webbed claws. As the flag fluttered in the breeze it seemed to make the sea monsters come to life. Indeed, as they stared up at it, the monsters heads appeared to turn towards them and open their jaws to exhibit large rows of shiny, razor-sharp teeth.

Zach tried to bring Abi and Izzie back to the matter in hand as he pointed out to them both, the alligators swimming menacingly around in the castle moat. Abi however, continued to stare up at the flag somewhat transfixed. As she stood there, Millie sat agitatedly by her side looking up at her, whilst making small, anxious whimpering noises and tamping her paws on the ground. Abi didn't seem to notice. It was Izzie, surprisingly, who was alert enough to see and point out a large sign above the inner gate on the far side of the moat that read:

VISITORS PLEASE RING THE BELL

A few yards to their left there was a very large bell mounted on a wooden jib. Zach grabbed the rope and gave it a good loud clang. A heavy wooden drawbridge started slowly to descend.

~ CHAPTER FIVE ~

The Castle

Once the drawbridge was in position they made their way across to the castle entrance. Either side of the doorway there was a sentry box, each containing a large figure dressed in armour with a sword by its side and a pikestaff in its right hand. The visors were down over their faces and neither of them made any movement. It was hard to tell if they were real people or not. Abi stepped forward and gave a sharp, hard pull on the metal handle which rang the inner doorbell.

Almost immediately they heard footsteps getting slowly louder and then the door swung open. There, stood a very tall, thin man in what looked like an old-fashioned butler's uniform with tails to his jacket, a bow-tie and white, cotton gloves. He had a pair of dark glasses on and a long, white stick in his left hand. The military style cap on his head had a badge with the word 'Equerry' pinned onto it. He was stood right in front of them as he looked out over their heads.

'Who has wrung the Summoner's bell?' he said in a very deliberate voice.

'We are Abigail Storm, Zachary Storm, Isabella Storm and Millie the dog and we have come to sign in as visitors as instructed,' said Abi.

'How do I know you are visitors?'

'Well we don't live here do we, so we must be visitors,' said Abi.

'Yes but do you have an invitation from the Summoner?'

'No,' said Abi getting more and more exasperated. 'The sign said 'ALL' visitors should sign in. It did not say only visitors with an invitation from the Summoner should sign in.'

'Yes, but do you have an appointment with the Summoner?'

'Oh, tish and tosh,' said Izzie pulling herself up to her full height, which because of her age wasn't really any height at all.

'No, we don't have an invitation or an appointment with the Summoner, whoever that might be. We are just following the rules which said we had to sign in at the castle.'

'Yes, but did the Herald issue you with an invitation?'

'Oh my godfathers,' said Izzie. 'No, no, no. We have never met the Herald. We are unheralded, maybe it's his day off, who knows, but could we just come in and have a bit of a rest and maybe a little something to eat?'

The Equerry stood silently for a few seconds as he weighed up the alternatives.

'This is most irregular but you may come in and wait while I consult the Summoner and see what the exact rules are for those who have not been issued an invitation by the Herald. Follow me.'

With that he turned, and it became clear by the way he felt around for the walls that he was indeed blind, which explained why he hadn't looked at them directly. They followed him down a long corridor with various flights of spiral, stone staircases leading upwards off of it. At the far end, he led them into a room which had a large table in the middle with about a dozen chairs around it.

'Wait there,' he said pointing at the table. As they sat down he went over to the right-hand wall and gave a very deliberate tug on a wire labelled 'Kitchen'. They could hear a bell ring below stairs and seconds later the sound of stomping feet getting louder and louder until a woman emerged out of a door in the corner and eyed them suspiciously.

'Yeah, whatcha want?' she shouted in a rather gruff voice. The Equerry just ignored her tone and pointing towards the table where they sat, asked her in a very calm, polite voice if she could please fetch them something to eat and drink. He then turned and went back out of the door they had come in through. The cook was wearing a rather grubby, white hat and a heavily stained apron and was carrying a large, metal ladle in her right hand.

'Three of you is there? Well whatcha want?' Izzie, didn't seem at all put off by the cook's coarse, short-tempered manner.

'Tea and cakes would be nice and could you bring something for our dog?'

'Tea and cakes, tea and cakes. I'll tea and cakes ya. More than my job's worth to give some of the Summoner's tea and cakes to just anyone, never mind the likes of you. Tea and cakes is for them that 'has' see. I've got a little mutton soup. You can have that and I'll fish the bone out for the dog.' With that she turned and disappeared downstairs again.

She had only just left when the other door opened and in came a smartly dressed and well-groomed lady in a twin piece suit. She looked oddly out of place with very large, oversized spectacles and heavy lipstick on a small but full-lipped mouth, perched on rather sucked in cheeks.

She carried a notepad and pen in her hand and, introducing herself as the Secretary, asked them for their names. Abi replied that they had already given their names to the Equerry when they arrived.

'Yes,' she said. 'The Equerry is a very kind and

decent man, but a little forgetful at times. He realizes that he forgot to write them down and has asked me to get your names for him so that he can give them to the Summoner.'

'Fiddlesticks,' said Abi. 'Why can't you just give them to the Summoner?'

'I can't, I'm not allowed to go into the Summoner's office or speak to the Summoner. Only the Equerry is allowed to do that.'

'But that doesn't make any sense,' said Abi. 'Why is it that only one person is allowed to enter the Summoner's office and speak to him?'

'Ah, the Summoner explained that to us when he made the appointment. He reminded us that he dealt with such delicate matters that if there were ever a leak or some sort of scandal we would all be suspects. That being so, he explained it would be better for us if none of us ever entered his office, except for the Equerry, who wouldn't be able to read any of his documents or see what the Summoner was doing and therefore would be above suspicion. We are all very pleased that the Summoner had our best interests at heart. That's the sort of man he is.' Abi rolled her eyes in dismay.

'Abigail Storm, Zachary Storm and Isabella Storm and the dog's name is Millie and no, we haven't got an invitation, we didn't meet the Guide and we didn't speak to the Herald either. We are just here to sign in as instructed.' With that the lady wrote down their names asking whether it was Zackary with a 'k' or Zachary with an 'h' and did Storm have an 'e' on the end and was Millie spelt Milly with a 'y' or Millie with an 'ie'.

'Excellent. I shall make arrangements and you will meet with the Summoner after you have eaten.'

'I thought no-one but the Equerry could meet the Summoner?' said Abi.

'Oh no, visitors can and indeed must meet the Summoner to be given his approval or otherwise. You are not allowed in his office however, so you will meet him in the visitor's meeting room at the top of stair six. I will take you there when the time comes.'

Just as she said this and turned to leave, the cook appeared at the top of the kitchen stairs carrying a tray with three soup bowls and a large bone on it. She placed the soups on the table with three spoons and threw the bone under the table for Millie. The soup was a watery, greyish-yellow colour, like something out of a washing up bowl. Zach tentatively dipped his spoon in, sniffed it a little and took a mouthful. He was soon dipping his spoon in again and it wasn't long before all three of them were scraping out their bowls and feeling full and satisfied.

Soon afterwards they were following the Secretary up staircase six to the visitor's meeting room. She knocked on the door. There was quite a long pause after which they heard a somewhat agitated sounding 'Enter'. They were a little hurriedly ushered in and the door was closed sharply behind them.

'Sit, sit,' he said without looking up. There were

three chairs ready for them and they each took a seat. Millie lay down just behind the door, still carrying her bone.

A man was sat at a very large desk with trays of paperwork and many splendid looking gold objects on it. There was a pen and ink stand, which had a sea nymph pattern, and a set of paperweights in the form of what looked like mythical serpents of various sizes.

He, like the Secretary, looked rather strangely out of place in modern clothes in an ancient castle. His suit was a little on the snug side for his slightly portly, rounded figure. His tie was light blue with gold thread running through it and seemed to match the long drapes behind him. They were in the same blue with gold sea serpents embroidered on them.

On the walls all around the room there were portrait paintings of rather austere looking men and women, presumably his predecessors. One painting was larger than the others and was hung on its own just behind and to the right of where he was sat. It was of the same fierce looking woman who appeared on the flag at the top of the castle.

As he raised his head, the first thing to note was that he had a face that could only be described as having a smirk where a smile should be. The smirk exposed two rather long, sharp pointed teeth, one either side of his mouth. It was a large mouth, thick-lipped and loose, perfectly in keeping with the fat, double chin that hung below it. However, it was his eyes that were his most striking feature in that they didn't show any warmth at all. Abi got the distinct feeling that rather than looking at them, the Summoner was looking down on them.

'Well, well, well. What do we have here? You do realise it is an offence to arrive without an invitation. I, and only I, issue them and to arrive without one and not be met by the Herald is strictly against the rules.'

'Well, if you didn't summon us here, then someone else must have done,' Abi said in a rather haughty voice.

'That's impossible,' he replied. 'I am the only person with the authority to summon visitors.' Abi came straight back at him.

'If you are the only person who can summon visitors then you must have summoned us. So, by your own admission, as we haven't got an invitation and the Herald didn't meet us, you must have broken your own rules. What's the point of rules if you break them yourself?'

'Cockamamie and strumplebum! Everybody knows that the first rule is that the Summoner can break the rules if he decides it is in the best interests of everyone to do so. That was the first rule I introduced on becoming Summoner. If I had to follow all the rules all the time I'd never get anything done and that wouldn't help anyone at all now would it?'

'Oh tish and tosh,' said Izzie for the second time that day. 'If the person who makes the rules doesn't have to follow them, how unfair is that? How can you expect everyone else to follow the rules if you're the only one allowed to break them? We didn't ask to come here, we didn't want to come here and if you could just show us the way home we can be on our way.'

'I'm afraid the rules won't allow that. As you have no invitation from the Herald you are not officially here and, if you're not officially here, I can't sign you a permit for your return home. Those are the rules.' He poured himself a goblet of wine from a decanter on his desk and sat back in his throne-like chair with an even more pronounced smirk on his face.

'Yes but you are in charge of the rules,' said Abi. 'You said yourself that you can change them at the drop of a hat whenever you want, can't you, and that's the truth of it, isn't it?'

'The truth! The truth!' the Summoner spluttered. 'It will only lead to trouble if you go about telling the truth. You can't run things and have a civil society if people keep on pointing out the truth and going on about unfairness. All it does is cause trouble and upset people. I mean everything can't be fair all the time, that's not natural.' Abi looked him straight in the eye with a sharp accusatory stare.

'Well, everything seems pretty fair for you all the time with your great big castle and making and breaking whatever rules you like and you don't seem to mind it. Your privileged life is the same for you from day to day. I am sure if everyone else had their fair share of the finer things in life then they wouldn't mind it either. They wouldn't mind it one bit.'

The Summoner's face reddened as his voluminous

jowls seemed to take on a life of their own.

'I am the Summoner,' he blurted out. 'I have my own needs and desires that I gladly sacrifice to live this life of burden and responsibility for the good of all. I will not have it, I will not have it. Guards, guards!'

The two figures who they had seen in the sentry boxes came shuffling their way into the room. In the sentry boxes they had looked rather scary and imposing but they entered in such a haphazard manner that Izzie couldn't help but giggle at the sight of them. Then, all of a sudden, the one in front's visor slammed down shut with a clang which startled him so much that he stumbled forward and hit his head on a large cabinet. The shock made him step back sharply into the other guard who then fell backwards, tripping over his own sword and landing with a loud crash on his rear end.

Izzie couldn't help herself and her giggles turned into raucous laughter. What made her laugh even more was when the guards began to weakly apologise to each other in a most bizarre fashion.

'Oh sorry, really sorry, sorry about that,' said guard one.

'No, no, my fault sorry, my fault,' insisted guard two. Her laughter made the Summoner even angrier.

'Take them to the cells. You need to learn respect for your betters and elders and have a care for the true ways of the world.' Abi still wouldn't let it go.

'But surely, if as you say we are not here officially and you can't sign a permit for us to return home then by the same token, you can't officially send us to jail?'

The Summoner had reached the end of his debating skills and simply made a dismissive hand gesture.

'Bah, I am the Summoner, I can do what I like to safeguard the people. The truth indeed. Take them away.'

The guards lined them up, one in front of the other, with Abi holding Millie by her lead, still with her bone in her mouth, followed by Izzie and then Zach. One guard then went at the front with the other at the back behind Zach. They marched them out of the room and down the corridor to the spiral staircase.

They were almost at the bottom of the stairs when Millie made a dash between the front guard's legs. Her lead tangled around them and brought him crashing down onto the floor of the main corridor below. Izzie and Zach quickly followed Abi down the last few steps, just in time to help her stretch Millie's lead across the bottom of the stairway. When the second guard came charging down he tripped over the lead and flew right across the main corridor, hit his head on the opposite wall and landed with a great thud on top of the first guard.

They all ran for the front door and soon had it open. As they dashed out, they suddenly realised that the drawbridge was up and they couldn't risk going back to lower it. Not wishing to end up as the alligators' afternoon snack they looked around desperately for another way out. Zach suddenly noticed that Millie still had her bone in her mouth. He grabbed it from her and ran down the far end of the moat waving it around so that the beasts would follow.

'Go, go!' he shouted and Abi and Izzie, with Millie just behind them, dived into the moat and swam as fast as they could to the other side. When Zack saw that Abi and Izzie were safely across and helping to haul Millie out of the water, he hurled the bone into the furthest corner of the moat. He then dashed back as fast as he could and followed them over just in time, before the snappers could swallow him up.

Not knowing whether the guards might follow, they quickly moved into a nearby glade, out of sight of the castle. There they sat, recovering their breath and drying themselves in the sun.

~ CHAPTER SIX ~

Abigail's Story

'What ho my fine fellows! I thought I'd never see the day. How will the world turn next?' The words came from somewhere a little way behind them. They spun round to see the broad, friendly smile of Will o' Castle Acre as he was dismounting from his horse.

'Never see what day?' said Izzie

'Escaping from the castle like that. Now there's a story to tell. Never seen anything like it. To escape from Aquavena by swimming the moat, oh the irony of it. Unbelievable, just simply unbelievable. She'll be wild with rage when she finds out.'

'Aqua who?' said Izzie, with a puzzled look on her face.

'Aquavena, the queen of all the waters of the oceans,

seas, lakes and rivers. She whose flag flies at the top of the castle,' he replied. 'This is her domain, but enough of her for now. Whom do I have the honour of addressing for the second time this fine day?'

'Abigail, Zachary and Isabella but please call us Abi, Zach and Izzie as our friends do,' said Zach. Having met Will again, Zach had concluded that he was the only person they had come across so far that they could trust and rely on and, that it would be a good thing to have someone they could trust and rely on.

'Abi, Zach, Izzie, will you join us for supper and some rest, you must be hungry and tired?'

'I am sure we would all like that,' Zach replied as Abi and Izzie each gave a thankful smile of relief for the offer.

'You said join 'us', who is 'us'?' said Abi.

Will gave a short, sharp, piercing whistle and a man and a woman on horseback suddenly materialised out of the long reeds of the fen trailing three horses behind them.

The man was tall and lean with a grey, tussled beard and moustache and hair of the same colour that fell around his ruddy, time-worn face. Although lean, he gave the impression of strength by the way he held himself in the saddle. His most striking feature was his deep blue eyes which were constantly patrolling every aspect of his surroundings with a sort of dignified wariness. That being said, the corners of his mouth gave the impression that, given the right circumstance, he would readily break into a smile that could warm the coldest of hearts. He raised a hand in a salute of welcome and in a soft, low voice with a hint of an accent from somewhere in the Low Countries, he introduced himself.

'Nico, Nico Dobben, at your service.'

The woman was younger with dark, plaited hair and a ready smile. She had a tartan, plaid swept around and pinned at the shoulder by a large, ornate silver brooch with a dark blue stone in the centre. The cloak was held in at the waist by a leather belt which had a sheath attached. In the sheath was a large knife with a deer's-horn handle encrusted with semi-precious stones and a solid silver, thistle-shaped hilt.

'Isla, Isla McClean from the land of Alban, pleased to meet you.' She had a majestic look about her in a wild, romantic way, as if she had been born in the saddle, ready-formed for cavalier acts of daring do.

'Honoured to make your acquaintance,' she continued. 'Your brave hearts are welcome, most welcome.' It was clear from her dress and her accent that she was from somewhere in the far, far north and wherever they might be now, there was something in the lilt in her voice and the light in her eye that made it clear that her heart still lay in her homeland.

As they dismounted and untied a horse for each of them, Abi thanked them both for their warm welcome and then made it clear to Will that none of them had ever ridden a horse before. He was quick to reassure them all that the horses were kindred spirits and knew exactly what to do so they need not worry. They helped each of them in turn to mount up and finally passed a very confused and befuddled looking Millie up to Zach for the ride.

They re-strung the horses together and slowly moved off deeper into the fen. As they rode along, after their long and exciting day, Abi became hypnotised by the slow and gentle rhythmic rocking back and forth motion of the horse beneath her. Her mind became dreamily detached from her surroundings and she suddenly found herself transported back in time and place to a summer's day in Downham when she was only five years old.

***

She was walking over the pretty bridge down near the flour factory. Her father, ever the educator, had told her many times that it was called Hythe bridge but when you are five years old and a bridge is covered in flowers, well 'the pretty bridge' it is.

She remembered that day, walking over the bridge on the right-hand side as you walk out of town towards Nordelph, with her and Millie some twenty yards or so behind the rest of the family. It was a warm, sunny day and the scent from the hundreds of beautiful, perfumed flowers that adorn the bridge each summer was making her feel woozy and light-headed. She was running a stick along the metal railings that allowed even the smallest of children to look down into the waters below in safety.

She was counting the rails as she went.

'One hundred and thirty-seven, one hundred and thirty-eight, one hundred and thirty-nine.'

Just as she reached the one hundred and fortieth rail, directly above the middle of the second span of the bridge, something extraordinary caused her to stop and stare straight down onto the calm, sunlit waters. There, between her and the water surface, were three vivid blue lights, each about the size of a tennis ball. They were in V formation, with one on its own in front and two behind, one on either side. They were travelling at speed and making a bee-line straight down the channel heading north towards King's Lynn. Abi looked all around and up in the sky above her to see if there was anything like an aeroplane or helicopter that could be causing the lights, but the sky was sunny, cloudless and empty and there was no-one else nearby.

This all seemed to happen in a matter of seconds and as the lights moved twenty to thirty yards or so down the channel they disappeared causing her to look back down again at the waters directly below her. It was then she saw three very large, shadowy figures under the water moving at great speed. The figures appeared together in the same V formation as the lights and in the same position in the channel in the middle of the second span of the bridge.

At the front was what looked like a very large, sinuous, aquatic beast with a shiny head and long, flowing body. It was followed by two similarly very large, very dark and scary looking creatures that reminded her of the skeletons of strange, ancient, aquatic animals her dad had shown her on a day out at the Natural History Museum in London. The three were swimming at speed underwater in perfect formation. Abi stared in amazement.

The rest of the family had reached the end of the bridge and were waiting patiently for her. They knew she was perfectly safe on her own, being protected by railings on both the water and the road side of the bridge and they also knew how she loved to linger and stare into the waters of the fen. It gave them all a little time to rest, so no-one was complaining.

All of a sudden Millie, who was also gazing down at the scene below, let out a horrendous, long howl followed by wild barking. Mr Storm stayed with the young ones while Mrs Storm came dashing back across the bridge to see what could possibly have happened to cause such a commotion.

Abi knelt down to try to calm Millie and comfort her. As she did so, she fancied she saw through the railings a long, thin watery arm appear out of the channel and a bony finger pointing back up at her. Abi held up the palm of her hand in response to the bony finger. She didn't know why she did that, but it just seemed the right thing to do.

In an instant, just where the arm had been, a beautiful swan suddenly rose up out of the water. It was a magnificent sight as it stood proud of the surface, flapping its mighty wings. The beads of water that flew off in all directions formed a spectacular, multi-coloured halo of light all around it. For a full ten seconds or more it seemed to be stood on the water, looking back towards the bridge. Then, with a mighty sweep of its wings it dived back down below the surface and disappeared out of sight into the darkness below.

When her mother got to her, Abi gave her a long-winded and fully detailed account, in the way five-year-olds do, of what she had seen and what had upset Millie. Her mother sympathized, and gave appropriate motherly hugs and comforting words to both of them. Having seen or heard nothing unusual herself, she was of the opinion that her young offspring was, as usual, somewhat prone to exaggeration. Already one of the most imaginative of children, she had probably seen ripples in the water, catching the sunlight, and put two and two together to make five.

***

As Abi rode along all of this came flooding back to her and she began to realise why she had stared at the flag on top of the castle for so long. Now that she thought about it, she was almost certain that the painting of the lady with the shiny, gold crown that hung in the visitor's meeting room, had a shield in the bottom left-hand corner with three vivid blue shapes on it. In the bottom right-hand corner was a magnificent swan, standing upright out of the water, with its wings fully spread. Unfortunately, she hadn't paid enough attention at the time to notice what the blue shapes were.

She began to wonder if this was not the first time she had crossed paths with Aquavena.

~ CHAPTER SEVEN ~

The Camp

They rode on for around half an hour or so, heading for a tall, lone tree in the distance. When they reached it, a young woman who was sat in its lower branches, was clearly pleased to see them and greeted them all, most especially Millie, with a beaming smile. At the same time, she raised the palm of her right hand towards them and said 'zalta' to each of them. She looked around eighteen to twenty years old and stared a little quizzically at the newcomers. Abi, Zach and Izzie gave a small, shy nod of the head in return, whilst the others all greeted her with the same 'zalta' salute.

About ten yards or so past the tree they wheeled sharply to the left and rode straight into a particularly thick patch of tall reeds. The reeds closed in behind them and they emerged on the other side into a large, open area which had about two to three hundred small cob houses made chiefly of baked mud and straw. The houses were laid out in streets that were positioned around a larger central building. This central building seemed to be a hive of activity with much noise and industry taking place and people busying themselves with the routine of the day. It had several entrances, with a different kind of work being carried out at each one.

There was a kitchen with sacks of grain, fruit and vegetables being prepared, bread being baked and large metal pots bubbling and steaming over open fires. At another opening, blacksmiths were hammering red hot metal into shape, making a variety of necessary tools, fixings and horseshoes. Clothing was being washed and repaired in the laundry section and in another area, wood was being worked on to make everything from barrels and boxes to tables and chairs.

They dismounted and Nico then led the horses into a paddock, where food, water and shelter was on hand for them. The girl that was in the tree had followed them in and Will asked her if she would go and summon the Council members to assemble in the Council chamber.

Ten minutes later Abi, Zach and Izzie were sat at a large table with Millie on her lead by their side. With them were Will, Nico, Isla and two other men and three other women, making eight members of the Council in all. They ranged in age from the youngest, who looked to be in her early twenties, to the oldest who was a kindly looking man with a grey beard and moustache that naturally suited his rather weather-beaten face.

They were sat in a circle around a table that had nothing to mark it out as anything other than a perfectly everyday, round wooden table. However, one chair was rather grander and slightly more ornate and elevated than the others. Sat in it was a man of about fifty years of age. He had a sign in front of him on the table which read:

Facilitator

He was distinguished by the fact that he had a red cloth with gold trim wrapped around his head. It hung down to one side of his face so that the trim just brushed against his cheek as he moved. He was also wearing a full-length, red robe that made him look as if he was ready for bed. Just to add to his flamboyant look, he had a monocle on his right eye which he fiddled with so often that Izzie, who had never seen anyone with a monocle before, wondered why he didn't wear spectacles instead.

He was holding what looked like the remains of an ancient somewhat scarred and broken paddle in his left hand and a book with a red cover with gold lettering on it in his right. He laid the book down on the table and put his right hand on it while still grasping the paddle in his left. His hands fully occupied, he was clearly having even more trouble controlling his monocle and the contortions on his face sent Izzie into a giggly fit that she was having great difficulty in controlling. When his face finally settled down, he cleared his throat and formally opened the meeting.

'The Council is now in session. All members shall follow the path of truth and justice and at all times conduct business in accordance with the rules and the guiding principles and commandments, as laid down by the founders in the Priscus Percepta. All say aye.'

When he finished, they all as one cried 'aye'. That done, he then said that those members of the Council who had not yet met the newcomers, should introduce themselves. He cocked his head to one side and wearing a broad grin, pointed a long, skinny finger at the sign in front of him.

'I am Professor Beaumont Devereaux Fitzjohn and I am the Facilitator.' Zach smiled to himself. If ever there was someone who clearly looked and acted like a mad professor with a mad professor's name, then Prof Beaumont Devereaux Fitzjohn fitted the bill perfectly.

'All that means is that I am in charge of making sure the meetings run smoothly according to the rules. Welcome to you all, including your dog, a Border terrier, if I'm not mistaken?' he added quizzically. Abi nodded.

With that he passed the paddle to the young lady on his right. In appearance she was in her early twenties and looked slim, fit and agile. There was no bright smile like the professor's. In fact she had a rather sullen expression on her somewhat mousey face. Her skin was of a slightly tanned complexion and short, winey-red coloured hair completed her sleek and nimble look.

'Roseanna Fox,' was all she said as she passed the paddle to the lady on her right. Zach once again noted that the person, Miss Fox, was well suited to her name. He wondered if looking like one's name was a trait everyone here shared, so he was interested to hear what the next lady had to say.

Zach immediately had her down as a dowager princess or someone's maiden aunt. She had a prim and proper air about her and wore pristine evening wear as if she was at an occasion. Indeed, Zach imagined that she would quite naturally see the Council meeting as an occasion that she should be appropriately dressed for.

She looked to be in her mid to late fifties. Every detail of her dress, her hair and her jewellery were coordinated to cultivate a style of easy and elegant sophistication. She took the paddle, and as she did so, turned and smiled at the lady on her right.

'We are Loretta and Lucille Bhat.' She then spelled it out to avoid any misunderstanding.

'B, H, A, T, – Bhat. We are the identical twin daughters of Colonel Somchai Panit Bhat, Lord High Commissioner to the King of Siam and Lady Millicent Rowbottom-Smythe, fifth cousin to the Duke of Windsor.'

'Thailand. It's now called Thailand dear,' said her sister Lucille. She then quickly followed that with 'Oh lummox, as my dear departed mother used to say, I forgot the bat. The bat dear, pass me the bat.' Loretta passed her the paddle.

'The paddle dear. We are to call it the paddle.'

'Oh yes, sorry dear, I meant the paddle, yes dear, sorry, sorry, the paddle.'

Zach eyed the two of them suspiciously. He couldn't decide whether they were a little hard of hearing or a few sandwiches short of a picnic. Or perhaps they were engaged in a well-rehearsed dance of verbal sparring, practiced over many years, in order to give the impression they didn't quite know what was going on even though they were fully alert and aware at all times.

Loretta looked at her sister disapprovingly as she held out her hand for her to return the paddle. As Lucille sheepishly handed it over, Zach studied Loretta's stern expression and the genuinely apologetic look on Lucille's face and decided that even the best actresses in the world couldn't pull that off. Accordingly, he came to the conclusion that the 'few sandwiches short of a picnic' option was by far the most likely. A marvelously, warm feeling of pleasure flooded over him as he scored his third hit in a row.

"As batty as Bhats," he thought to himself.

Loretta now had the paddle and realised almost immediately that she would have to pass it back to Lucille so that she could then pass it on to the man on her right. Not wishing to look foolish, having indicated she wanted the paddle returned to her when in reality she had nothing more to say, she fell back on her years of hosting grand receptions in the embassy and managed to conjure up a diplomatic smile.

'Welcome all,' she said and immediately passed the paddle back to Lucille.

'Yes, welcome, welcome, welcome from me too,' said Lucille. 'Oh and welcome to you too,' she said, casting an extra smile in Millie's direction. She then passed the paddle on to the elderly gent.

He was comparatively roughly clad, with heavy boots, a thick jumper and a woollen bobble hat with the design of a large, rowing boat stitched onto it. Most unusually, for Abi, Izzie and Zach, he had the noticeable feature of a wooden-bowled smoking pipe in the corner of his mouth, though it wasn't lit.

He took the paddle in his left hand and as he did so, removed the pipe from his mouth with his right. With his head bowed and his eyes on the table in front of him, he slowly rubbed the pipe's bowl against his brow as if he was thinking long and hard about something. He took a deep breath, which sounded more like a sigh, and lifted his head. As he did so, his eyes danced around in such a way that they seemed to fill the room with brightness and cheer, making him look much younger and livelier than he had at first appeared.

'I be Jago Jelbart, fisherman and lifeboat crewman from Penzance like. Ye can call me Jago. I be very pleased to meet ye all. I finds it kinda sad for ye be'en 'ere so young an' all but I'm sure ye will get used to it dreckly. If there be anything you need, just say. I'll do what I can, proper job like.'

Like a true Cornishman, and you could not get a truer Cornishman than Jago Jelbart, it wasn't really what he said or even the need to understand every word he said. It was more a feeling that if anyone was requiring help in any way, Jago would be there for them. He passed the paddle on to Isla and popped his unlit pipe back into his mouth. Putting his thumb over the top of the bowl he gave a long, satisfying draw and pop, which gave the impression that in his world, if you believed you were smoking a pipe then you were smoking a pipe and there was nothing Aquavena could do about it.

The paddle was then passed from Isla to Nico and finally on to Will, who was sat beside the Facilitator. He introduced Abigail, Zachary, Isabella and Millie in a more formal way and explained how he had come across them that morning. Then he told them of his astonishment when he had later seen them escaping from the castle by swimming across the moat. Even more unusually disturbing to the Council was the explanation that they had come through the Cauldron without the Guide and had not been announced by the Herald, making them, as far as he, or anyone else knew, the only non-summoned inhabitants of Maritania.

'Maritania? Where is Maritania?' said Abi on hearing the word for the first time.

'You cannot speak without the speaker's paddle,' said Roseanna, having stood up and leaned across the Facilitator to snatch it from Will. She handed it back to him and Will continued unperturbed.

'Why this is Maritania, here, where you are now. It is the land ruled by Aquavena who is the queen of the all the waters of the oceans, seas, lakes and rivers. It seems each of us has been summoned to live for the rest of eternity, here in her hidden realm.'

'Well we weren't summoned,' said Abi in a very determined way. Roseanna was immediately on her feet again.

'Even the Summoner agreed we weren't summoned so we won't be staying here. Thanks for your hospitality and all that but there has obviously been some sort of mistake so we will be leaving as soon as it is light in the morning.'

'Excuse me,' said Roseanna, having leaned across and clutched the paddle out of Will's hand for a second time. 'You cannot speak without the speaker's paddle. It is the Council, and only the Council, who will decide what will and will not happen, not you.'

'Poppycock,' said Abi. 'We won't be told what to do by a Council we've never heard of in a land we never wanted to come to. You might as well tell fish they can't swim or birds they can't fly as tell us what we can and cannot do.'

'Ah ha,' said the young lady again. 'She speaks of telling fish not to swim. How do we know they are not scrones? It seems quite incredible that all three of them swam the moat without being caught. No-one else has ever managed that. Sounds too good to be true. Only scrones could swim that fast. Of course it could all be a trick and they were allowed to escape the castle and swim the moat so that we would take them in and give them shelter. Then, they could spy on us and report back to the Summoner.'

'Seems to me,' said Abi 'it's you that acts like those in the castle. The Summoner is full of lies and deceit and twists the truth to suit his ends. He makes the rules for others and doesn't bother to follow them himself. His actions erode decency and trust, so much so that it can soon become quite normal for others to do the same and before long, not very long at all, it is difficult to tell the difference between lies and the truth and right and wrong.

'As for your paddle, well hocus pocus, myth and magic. It's just another way to subvert the human spirit and keep people in order. All this ritual and ceremony is designed to strip the individual of their uniqueness in the world. One more way to keep everyone subservient and in their place.'

With that Will again took the paddle from Roseanna and asked that now they had been introduced, as is the long tradition for new citizens, would the Council agree to him being responsible for their safekeeping for the time being. He promised to keep them well-cared for and secure and to explain further to them the ways and customs of the world they were now living in. The Council took an open show of hands vote and, being a long-standing, well-respected member of the Council, they all found in Will's favour.

The Facilitator, then turned to Abi, Zach and Izzie.

'As our newest arrivals, in accordance with the ancient tradition, you will be our guests of honour at the next Lunatum.' He paused, smiled deeply and then added, 'Of course we would be greatly honoured if Millie would attend also. There is nothing to fear. I am sure Will, Isla and Nico will explain the Lunatum to you.'

Isla smiled at them reassuringly. The Facilitator then put his right hand on the red book, and with the paddle in his left hand, formally closed the meeting.

Will, Nico and Isla took the three of them, plus Millie, to the refectory. It was obvious they were by far the youngest people there and news of their arrival, without an official summoning, raised the interest in them beyond that normal for newcomers. Isla made it her business to make sure they each had a good helping of food. She also showed an openness and a warmth to them that encouraged others to come over and meet them, say hello and make them feel welcome. However, it appeared that the main reason others came over to greet them was to meet Millie. A dog was a unique novelty and one as cute as Millie soon became the centre of attention.

~ CHAPTER EIGHT ~

Isla's Story

After their meal Zach and Millie went with Will to his house where they were to stay the night, while Abi and Izzie, having said goodnight to him, went with Isla. They were soon sat in her living room, each with a small mug of a slightly warm, frothy drink which Isla assured them would help them get a restful night's sleep after their long, tiring day.

As they sipped at their nightcaps, they stared around at the pictures on the walls which depicted, mountains and deep lakes, dramatic headlands and cliffs, castles and wild countryside filled with herds of majestic stags and grazing highland cattle. Alongside the pictures were a large pair of crossed broadswords and a leather shield bearing on it a design in the form of Celtic knots.

On the far wall hung a large tattered flag, white with a red cross on the left-hand side and the lion rampant on the right-hand side. It had the head of a king with his crown in the very centre.

As their eyes tired, Isla guided them through to where they were to sleep. Once they had lain down, she sat on the end of Izzie's bed and told them her tale.

***

As a young girl, long, long ago in the land of Alban far to the north, I lived with my mother and father in the Great Glen on the banks of the river Enrick. Our family were simple sheep farmers and scratched a living out of the thin mountainous pastures.

My job was to walk the hillsides amongst the sheep with a whirling stone to frighten off the eagles who would occasionally swoop down from the mountains to carry off the lambs to feed to their young. I would spin the whirling stone on a piece of string around my head and then let it go so that the stone flew hard and fast at the eagles. In no time at all I got very accurate with the stones and it wasn't long before my presence alone, whirling the stone around my head, was enough for them to fly off without reward for their efforts.

One day my father was taking his boat out fishing in nearby Loch Ness. He took me with him and set me to work patrolling the sheep on the lower pasture near the loch. Having worked all morning I went down to the shore and sat on a large, flat stone to eat my lunch. As I sat there, I watched my father cast his rod and reel in the fish we would be eating that evening.

I was nearly finished the bread, fruit and small piece of oatcake my mother had baked for me, when there suddenly appeared, about one hundred yards or so from my father's boat, a monstrous, scaly beast about twenty yards long with three humps on its back. It had a long, thin neck and a small head and was travelling smoothly at great speed, heading straight for him. I shouted out as loud as I could but he was too far away to hear me.

The monster was getting closer and closer, still heading for him so, in desperation, I loaded my whirling stone, spun it as hard as I could and let fly. The stone fairly flew out across the waters at lightning speed and caught the beast hard on its forehead right between the eyes. As it hit, the monster reared up and let out a great wail of pain and then dived deep under the waters and disappeared into the murky depths.

That night, as I lay sleeping, I was visited by an evil looking woman with a long cape and a crown on her head. She told me I would regret attacking one of her creatures from the deep, who were the beloved servants of her realm. She stood over me and delivered this warning.

'I, Aquavena, queen of the waters of all the oceans, seas, lakes and rivers warn you that if you ever cross me again you will be cursed forever more.'

Years went by and I grew up into a strong, independent woman. When duty called, without hesitation, I went to fight for King and country. I joined the King's cavalry in Edinburgh and was soon heading south to face Cromwell's army near the border at Dunbar. Unfortunately the King's army was heavily defeated and I was captured and held prisoner in Durham Cathedral. From there I was marched down south with the rest of the defeated army, to the great flooded wetlands of Norfolk. There, we were set to work day after day digging out huge drainage channels to lower the water-table and return the sunken land from the seas.

I was housed in a large barn with scores of other prisoners, in Barroway Drove on the outskirts of Downham Market. It was there I met Nico, who was a gunner on a Dutch galleon and had been captured by the British navy after the sinking of his ship.

I first struck up a friendship with Nico when we were detailed to go once a week into the market in Downham to help load the carts with supplies for the camp. Although it was hard work stacking the heavy boxes of food and barrels of liquid onto the carts, I looked forward to it as it was a change from digging out mud all day while being prodded and harassed by the guards out on the fen. The other reason I liked to go into town was that the local townsfolk of Downham were not in favour of the draining of what was their fishing grounds, where they earned their livelihood. They therefore felt sorry for us, being forced to live a great distance away from our homelands and carry out the backbreaking work. Indeed they hated the guards and pitied the prisoners so much that when I was in the town, they would occasionally sneak me a small treat, such as a piece of cake or a little fresh fruit. I would hide any such little gifts under my cloak and take them back to share with the others in the camp.

Nico and I soon grew a strong bond of friendship. Being much older and more experienced in the ways of the world, he kept a watchful eye open for me and helped me cope with the rough life we led.

I didn't know it at the time but, in his earlier years, Nico had helped design and build the sea defences in his native Netherland. For daring to hold back the waters of the Great North seas, he too had been visited in the night by Aquavena to be warned of her curse if he ever crossed her again. So it was, that without either of us knowing it, both Nico and I had received the same warning.

One day, when we were both out on the fen with a team digging a new drain between Nordelph and March, a great storm swept in from the North Sea and sent a high tide speeding down the Wash into the Great Ouse river. A huge wave of water came rushing down the Middle Level Drain and forced itself into the much narrower Sixteen Foot Drain, the one we were working in. As it did, it became a great wall of water that in a matter of seconds swept right over us. It was so powerful that several of our companions were instantly drowned in the swirling waters. Nico, having been a sailor, and I having been brought up on the banks of the great loch, were both strong swimmers and managed to make it to higher ground and save ourselves.

That night however, as I lay in my bed sleeping, Aquavena, having failed to drown me, visited me for a second time. She stood over me and reminded me of her warning.

She said that in draining the fen and turning the seas into dry land, I had stolen a part of her realm and as this was the second time I had dared to cross her, I must now pay the price. With that she held out her sword over me and carried out the curse.

'I, Aquavena, queen of all the waters of the oceans, seas, lakes and rivers from this time forth banish you to the land of Maritania for the rest of eternity.'

Aquavena then visited Nico and carried out the same curse on him. From that time forward Nico and I have found ourselves trapped in the land of Maritania, unable to escape ever since.

***

Having finished her story Isla got up from the bed.

'That was my story,' she said. 'I hope it has helped you to understand some of the strangeness that surrounds you.' She then bent over each of them in turn and tucked them in so that they were covered and comfortable, blew out the candles and bid them a soft goodnight.

'Goodnight,' they both replied.

Abi lay there for a minute or two taking in all the weird events of the day and pondering over Aquavena and the happenings in Isla's story.

'You alright Izzie?' Abi asked in a caring, reassuring way, but Izzie was already far, far away in the land of nod.

~ CHAPTER NINE ~

The Hunt for Polly

Early the next morning Will woke Zach and, after breakfast, asked him if he would like to go hunting with him.

'Hunting what?' said Zach, thinking that he had never been hunting before and couldn't see himself killing an animal unless it was to defend himself or protect someone being attacked.

'Why, the two things I always go hunting for. My Polly of course, the sweetest maid in all the world, and then, and only then, the gateway out of this land back to my home and family and friends in Castle Acre. I must find them both for I will never return home without my Polly.'

'How do you know that Polly is here in this land?'

asked Zach.

'Oh she is here somewhere,' said Will. 'I have no doubt about that. On the day I was summoned here, the Summoner told me my fate and, although I had never mentioned her to him, he said I would never see Polly in Maritania no matter how long I searched. I knew straight away that she must be here somewhere for why would he say that if she were not. As is often the case, those in the seat of power can get too clever for themselves sometimes. This is true in the real world and is no different here with the scrones. Apart from that I simply know in my heart that she is here somewhere. I fancy I can hear her cry out to me in the night and as long as I am here I shall never stop searching for her.'

Zach had heard the young woman at the Council talk about scrones so when Will repeated the word he asked him what it meant.

'Scrones are what we call the creatures from the deep that Aquavena has transformed into temporary human form to carry out the necessary procedures for the running of Maritania.'

'What do you mean?' said Zach not fully grasping what Will was telling him.

'Well for example, the Guardian is a seahorse and has to wear an eyepatch as he finds it too tricky with both eyes looking forward instead of one on either side of his head. The blind Summoner's Equerry is a transformed eel who is used to living in the dark recesses of the river bank. The cook is a crusty old crab, the kind that normally live their life crawling in and out from under rocks or from holes in harbour walls. The guards are all sharks. They can be vicious, though to be truthful they're not the brightest of fish in the sea. Then of course there's the Summoner, well he is a grumpy, old walrus who makes up rules and dishes out orders without any regard for the consequences to others.'

As soon as Zach understood Will's explanation of the scrones he immediately pictured in his own mind the Secretary and how she reminded him of an angel fish with her large, staring eyes and small mouth with sucked in cheeks and puckered up lips.

'What about Abi and Izzie?' said Zach. 'Will they be coming hunting with us?'

'No, no. Isla is going to look after them today and show them around the village and explain everything to them. Is that okay?'

'Yes, fine. I would like to come with you if you are sure that I won't be a hindrance to you on your search? Before we leave can I just let Abi and Izzie know and leave Millie with them while we're away?'

'Yes of course, I'll take you to them.' With that, Will picked up his jacket, hat and lute and made for the door.

'Come,' he said in a bright and cheery, optimistic fashion. 'I think you could bring me luck and today just might be the day.' Zach followed him out of the door. They went straight to Abi and Izzie and Zach made sure that they were happy for him to go with Will. He handed over Millie and then they went to get the horses and were soon saddled up and on their way. They went all the way through the village to the far side with Will giving the same right hand raised 'zalta' greeting to everyone they met.

They reached the far end and started to make their way through the tall reeds when Will turned in his saddle and leaning earnestly forward, gave Zach a most serious look.

'Keep your eyes and ears wide open and yourself alert. There is no telling what you might see or hear. Anything can happen at any time and the success or otherwise of our search might depend upon it.' Zach wasn't quite sure what he meant but by the manner in which he said it, he knew it was important. For some reason he found himself saying 'aye' as if that was the expected appropriate response.

Seconds later Zach couldn't believe his eyes. As they came out of the reeds, there in front of them was a beach, a golden stretch of sand leading down to a swirling, foaming sea with waves rolling in and lapping up the shore towards them. There was a fresh breeze and over their heads, seagulls were wheeling and diving while gannets and razorbills, who lined the rocky escarpments on either side of the bay, plunged headlong into the shiny, blue waters.

Then, Zach sat stock still in wonder and amazement when his eyes alighted upon a three-masted galleon which lay halfway between the shore and the horizon. It was too far away to make out any detail on the deck but there was no mistaking the flag that flew atop the main mast. Along its bows, in large gold letters it read:

THE LEVIATHAN

Zach just sat and stared, unable to take his eyes off of it.

'Aquavena,' he said under his breath as if he dare not say the word out loud.

'We believe so,' said Will. 'We understand it to be her lair but we have never been near enough to know for sure. It is surrounded by sharks, giant octopuses and all manner of sea monsters too dangerous to confront. Occasionally small boats go back and forth from the ship to a cave on the edge of the cliff which must be the underground route directly into the castle. We think it is how they refresh supplies and bring new scrones in to relieve the current ones. It's likely that the scrones can't stay out of the water indefinitely and need to be rested and replaced every now and then.'

They sat there a moment or two longer and then Will wheeled his horse to the left and moved off slowly along the shoreline. Zach and his mount automatically followed in behind.

After twenty minutes or so they reached a large rock where the path divided. Will turned left to go further inland and as he did so he let go of the reins, swung his lute round in front of him and started to sing a gentle little song:

'As I came riding in to Downham-o

As I came riding in to Downham -o

I fell in love

With a lady like a dove

Her name it was pretty Polly-o

Oh there's many a pretty maid in Southery

There's many a pretty maid in Denver-o

Oh there's many a heart to win

In the town of old Kings Lynn

But the flower of them all lives in Downham-o

She came riding through the fair pretty Polly-o

She came riding through the fair pretty Polly-o

Riding through St Winnold's fair

With red ribbons in her hair

The prettiest girl you've ever seen-i-o'

Zach, on hearing of Downham, once again became a little homesick and he wiped a small tear from the corner of his eye. They trotted on a mile or two more and then stopped to let the horses drink at a cool stream. As they did so, Will asked Zach if he would be happy to wait with the horses while he climbed up to the top of the rocks by the side of the path to see if he could see any sign of Polly from the higher ground. Will told him he would only be a few minutes so Zach agreed. He set off climbing higher and higher up the rocks until he reached the top. Once he got there,, he started to shout out over the countryside in a booming voice.

'P-o-l-l-yeeeee, P-o-l-l-yeeeee, P-o-l-l-yeeeee.'

The horses started to become agitated and whickered and pawed and scuffed at the ground. Zach grabbed at their reins and stroked them, trying his best to calm them down with gentle soothing words.

As he was doing so, something made him look up over to the other side of the stream. Just as he did, a large black wolf, with its head bowed, came loping out of the woods towards them. It hadn't noticed him at first but then it heard the horses and suddenly stopped in its tracks and fixed its sharp, bright green eyes directly on Zach. For a second or two it stood its ground and pulled its gums back to bare its teeth but then, no sooner had it done so, than it turned tail and trotted off back into the woods.

The sudden appearance, the staring green eyes and the blackness of its fur had startled Zach. He breathed a heavy sigh of relief and turned his attention back to the horses. Within a minute or two they had just settled down as Will re-appeared on the rock above them with his usual friendly smile and an air of resignation and acceptance.

'No luck, but the day is young. Everything okay Zach?' Zach smiled back at him as something inside of him told him to keep the wolf incident to himself.

'Yes, sorry you haven't found her.'

'Yet Zach! Haven't found her yet, and with four eyes rather than two we've doubled the chances. Let's go.' With that he jumped down and they mounted the horses and rode on.

~ CHAPTER TEN ~

Will's Story

They rode on for another hour with Will occasionally singing his songs. Every now and then he would pause to listen, or stare intently into the woods or longingly out across the open landscape of the fen. Then they dismounted in a small clearing and settled down to some food and drink that Will had produced from his saddlebags. The drink was the same as the one he had had the night before. It was a little bitter to taste but soon coursed through Zach's veins and emboldened him to ask Will more about who he was and how he had ended up in Maritania. Will was happy to tell him about it and as he did so, Zach sipped a little more of his drink and felt comfortable and safe.

***

WILL'S STORY

I was brought up by my mother and father, landlady and landlord of The Crown tavern in Castle Acre. My father taught me to shoot, hunt, fish and ride a horse as good as anyone in the county, and of course, how to brew and keep the very best of beer. My mother taught me civility, humility and, with the help of the monks in Castle Acre priory, how to read and write.

As a boy I had spent many happy hours playing with my friends in the ruins of the castle and that led me on to become interested in the castle's history. I studied all I could about the building of castles and similar large structures such as palaces and cathedrals.

Later, I was invited to attend the university in Cambridge to further my studies and there I learned how to draw up accurate plans for the construction of such buildings so that they would be strong and withstand the test of time. I gained a certain amount of recognition for the quality of my work and for introducing new and innovative ideas that resulted in speedier and more reliable building techniques. They reduced cost and at the same time increased reliability, so my designs began to find favour.

When they started the work to drain the fens, under the guidance of Dutch engineers who had done similar work in the Netherlands, they called on me to assist by drawing up design plans and overseeing the installation of a mechanical barrier to regulate the flow of water in the Great Ouse river at Denver.

My father was a good friend of the landlord of The

Rampant Horse tavern in the High Street at Downham Market and so it was, that while I was engaged in the work at Denver, I stayed for that time in an upstairs room in the Rampant Horse. I took my meals there and in the evenings supped good ale and enjoyed the company of the locals who frequented the tavern to meet and share their news and gossip after their hard days labour.

On one such night, when it was wet and windy outside, all of a sudden there was a disturbance at the tavern door as a woman in a long cloak and hood made a noisy entrance.

'Come father,' she cried, with a hint of laughter in her voice. 'Come else you'll be soaked right through.' As she said this, she helped the gentleman off with his cloak and hat and hung them up on the hanging rail and then dusted him down and straightened his clothing.

'Come, come you'll catch your death,' she said, ushering him in. 'Sit you down here by the fire and get warmed through.'

There was something in the manner of her voice and the way she spoke that immediately caught my attention. Once she had settled the man into his seat she returned to the front door rail, removed her cloak and then took off her bonnet. As she did so, long locks of shiny, black hair cascaded down her back and floated and danced around her shoulders. When she turned around I, already entranced, couldn't help but stare at the most beautiful young lady I had ever seen. She had startling green eyes and a smile that lit up the room. After a few seconds I had to tear my eyes away from her so as not to appear rude.

The locals all greeted her warmly. She settled her father in with a beer and once she had caught her breath, soon became engaged in merry chat with the landlady, full of smiles, giggles and knowing looks and winks.

'Come on young Polly dear, give us a song,' cried one of the men who was sat beside her father by the fire. All the rest of the company joined in urging her to sing and she waved her hands to quieten them down and then, without hesitation, she began to sing. The song she sang was 'The Rambling Boys of Pleasure' a lovely old Irish ballad she said she had learned from her mother, as a young girl, back in county Sligo.

She sang it with a voice as beautiful as the song itself and I was entranced. I had heard the song many times before but it had meant little to me. It was a song that warned young gentlemen against falling in love too quickly or too deeply but it was already too late, for at that very moment I was falling head over heels.

Polly became a regular visitor to The Rampant Horse. As the weeks went by we got to know each other better and it was plain we were very keen on each other. We became a bit of a favourite with the locals, with me playing the lute and Polly singing so beautifully and we were soon walking out together. Polly would sometimes ride out to Denver windmill and meet me on my way back to town at the end of the day and we would often stroll around the Howdale on a Sunday morning, taking the air.

Downham Market was the town where the biggest horse fair in England was held. It took place once a year, early in March, on St. Winnold's Day. Thousands of horses, that were the major source of transport at that time, were bought and sold with hundreds of people coming into the town for three or four days to get their pick of the mares and stallions on offer.

On the first day of the fair there was a ceremonial parade by the townsfolk to welcome all the traders and visitors to the town. They had a marching band at the front and they were followed by some of the town dignitaries in horse-drawn carriages. Behind them came a few of the well-known characters of the town, of whom Polly was one.

She had groomed her glossy, black mare to look her very best. She then set her in a red bridle which she matched with red ribbons tied into her own similarly shiny, black hair. I was so proud of her as I waved her off before taking my place with the general throng at the rear of the parade.

We rode down Paradise Road, one or two of us tipping our hats to the gallows platform in memory of the odd soul who had gone astray for the last time.

We then rode out onto Bridge Street and back up towards the High Street and the Market Square.

When I arrived back in the square I was so in love with her that there and then I asked her to marry me and come and live with me in Castle Acre. She made me the happiest of men when she said yes and the wedding was set to take place as soon as the work on the sluice gate at Denver was completed.

When the opening day of the sluice came, there was much ceremony and I was given the honour of being the first to pull the levers to operate the gate that could control any high tidal surges of the Great Ouse river and so stop it from bursting its banks and flooding the newly created farmland out in the fen.

Despite all the congratulations and praise for the outstanding work we had done, all I could think about was Polly and the wedding day. I returned that night to my home in Castle Acre and went to bed happy that the work was over and soon I would be with Polly forever. I was sleeping soundly when, in the middle of the night, Aquavena visited me and said I must pay the price for the blocking of the waters and cutting off part of her realm. She then held out her sword over me and carried out the curse.

'I, Aquavena, queen of all the waters of the oceans, seas, lakes and rivers banish you to the land of Maritania for the rest of eternity.'

I have been searching for Polly ever since.

***

His story over, Will stood up, stretched his limbs and put a hand on young Zach's shoulder.

'But enough of me, what say you young man, on with our search?' Zach stood up, dusted himself down and made himself ready to move on.

'Before we do, can I ask why you greet each other with the word 'zalta'. What does it mean exactly?'

'Ah,' said Will. 'Well the scrones have great difficulty with the letter Z and indeed never use it, so we greet each other with 'zalta' as our way of checking that we are not talking to scrones.'

'If that's the case why did the young lady at the Council suspect we might be scrones when my name is Zach?'

'Ah Roseanna. Don't be fooled. She is a kind-hearted soul but sometime suspicion and fear can get the better of commonsense. We must forgive when it does. We are all prone to failings in our judgement from time to time and it's as well to remember that.'

Zach gave him a knowing smile, recognising similar failings in his own relatively short life. They mounted their horses and rode on.

~ CHAPTER ELEVEN ~

The Mountain of Dreams

They had been riding around fenland country for an hour or so when on the distant horizon Zach saw a huge mountain at least twice the height of any mountain he had ever seen before. Just as he noticed it he heard a great whooshing noise slowly getting louder and louder. He stopped and turned in his saddle to see a mass of fifty or so enormous eagles seemingly in formation coming their way, each with a huge squirming fish in its talons.

The eagles were heading for the mountain and provided a truly awesome sight as they flew overhead. Zach's first impression was one of wonder at the size, might and power of them as their giant wings beat the air with a steady, ear-deafening rhythm.

The majesty of the eagles was cruelly magnified by

the desperate plight of the fish. They too were majestic in their beautiful, streamlined, aquatic form, all silver and gold scales shimmering like giant jewels in the sunlight. Zach pitied them as he saw the look of terror in their eyes and felt their shock and pain at being hauled out of their world into an alien one, with no idea of their fate. A fate, Zach reflected, it was better for them not to know.

Will had doubled back to hold the reins of Zach's horse as he knew both horses would be spooked a little by the unusual sound of the eagles.

'You alright Zach?' Will said once the eagles had passed by.

'Yes. What do you call that place?' said Zach as he pointed at the mountain.

'That is the Mountain of Dreams.'

'Why is it called that?' said Zach.

'Because if you travel towards it, it slowly fades and the more you desperately try to reach it the faster it dissolves and disappears. Just like your dreams.'

Will handed back the reins to Zach and they started off again. Zach couldn't get the fish out of his mind. There they were, being hauled out of their own world and into a strange new one just as he had been. He saw the fear in their eyes and wondered at the fragility of it all, whilst counting his blessings that so far he had not ended up with a similar fate to theirs.

Meanwhile, back in the camp Abi and Izzie spent the day with Isla, who showed them around, answering as many of their questions as she could.

After a midday meal, knowing that their ability to ride horses at speed would be critical, Isla took them to the paddock where the horses were kept. Abi and Izzie had only ever been on a horse for the short time the day before as they were being brought to the camp.

Isla showed them how to saddle the horses, adjust the stirrups, sit correctly and use the reins for control. She also explained to them that there was mutual respect between the people and the horses. Both understood the sacrifices each were willing to make for the other in order to survive in harmony together. As long as they showed the horses love and kindness, the horses would treat them with the same respect and understanding.

Izzie chose the smaller piebald horse she had been on the day before while Abi, being Abi, decided she would go for the shiny, black stallion with a hint of menace and daring in its eyes.

Abi tied Millie to one of the rails and once they were mounted, they walked the horses round the circular track for a short while before Isla set them into a trot. She showed them how to slow and stop and then start again and go back into a trot. After only a short time trotting round, both of them began to feel the joy and the freedom of being at one with the most beautiful of beasts. So much so in fact that they both broke into a canter together and then began to gallop as if they had been riding horses all their lives.

Isla was taken aback but her anxiety was short-lived

as it became clear that they were both having the thrill of their lives and were fully in control, as if they were born to it. After three circuits, each one faster than the last, they eased off to a slow canter and then down to a trot before coming to a halt.

'I thought you said you had never ridden horses before?' Isla said in sheer disbelieve at how skilled and competent they were.

'I can assure you,' said Abi, her face beaming with the excitement and exhilaration of the ride, 'we have never ridden horses before. You must be an excellent teacher.'

After they dismounted, while Isla was leading the horses back to their paddock, Abi untied Millie from the rail and she and Izzie headed for a quiet corner where there were a few picnic tables, to rest and get their breath back. It was near to a thick patch of reeds that offered some shelter from a cooling breeze.

'Any idea what just happened there Izzie?' Abi said in low tones. 'I mean it's pretty strange how both of us could ride like the wind even though we have never ridden horses before?'

'I really don't know,' said Izzie. 'But then again everything seems strange here so I don't suppose we should be surprised.' Abi was impressed by Izzie's acceptance of their situation at such a young age. She understood that Izzie would have to grow up fast to deal with their new reality and was pleased to see she was making a good start at adjusting to it.

Abi had for some time now been wondering how to tackle Izzie on the reality of their situation. She didn't want to worry her, but at the same time she felt it would probably help her if they talked about it. So, as they sat down, she tentatively asked her how she was feeling and if there was anything she needed to talk about. Izzie's response was not what Abi was expecting.

'There is one thing worrying me. I feel that you know something about this place that you're not telling me. We've always shared everything with each other but now I'm getting the feeling that you're keeping something from me Abi.'

'Well yes, actually. I am fairly sure that I have come across Aquavena and the two creatures alongside her on the castle flag before. One day I was on the bridge over the relief channel at Downham when I think I saw all three of them swimming at speed under the water. I thought the creature in front had a shiny head but I now realise that it was almost certainly Aquavena's gold crown catching the sun. She seemed to raise an arm out of the water and point a finger at me and then she transformed into a beautiful swan, with large spreading wings, before diving back under the surface and disappearing out of sight.

'Everyone else here says that they were visited by her in their sleep and no-one seems to have actually seen her in the waters like I did. It makes me wonder if that might have something to do with why we are here. Maybe there is a special purpose behind our arrival? The fact that we have not been summoned seems to me to suggest that it is not Aquavena who has brought us here.

Perhaps it's somehow because of Will, Isla, Nico and the others instead. I mean I did think it a little strange that when we first met them they had three horses with them. One for each of us. Seemed rather odd. But then again everything is pretty strange here so there's no telling?'

Abi and Izzie were so close that Izzie was a little shocked at what she had just heard.

'Why haven't you told me about the bridge at Downham before Abi?'

'Well to be honest Izzie, it was a long time ago and I was very young. Soon after it happened it began to fade from my memory. In fact, until we came here I had convinced myself it might well have never happened at all, but now I am sure it did. What do you think? Do you think it's possible we might have been brought here on purpose to somehow help the others get back to where they belong?' Before Izzie had a chance to answer a familiar voice made them turn to see Zach coming to join them.

He was so excited that he lost no time in telling them about his adventures that day. Both Abi and Izzie were amazed when he described the beach, the sea, the galleon the Leviathan, and the cave that might lead to the castle. He then went on to explain the role of the scrones in running Maritania and finally, the Mountain of Dreams, the eagles with the fish and the big black wolf with the startling green eyes that scared the horses.

As if that wasn't enough, when each had told the other about Isla and Will's stories of how they and Nico had ended up there, what surprised them most of all was that each of them seemed to have some connection with Downham at the time they were summoned. That led on to Abi repeating her revelation about seeing Aquavena in Downham to Zach and wondering if somehow that was significant. He was just as surprised as Izzie and agreed that it could well have something to do with why they are there.

~ CHAPTER TWELVE ~

The Wolf Moon

It was the night of the January full moon, known as the Wolf Moon, and so it was that the next Lunatum had arrived. Will explained to them that they would follow at the back of the torchlit procession to the Sacred Ground where the ceremony would take place. He and Isla and Nico, who were their patrons, would walk just ahead of them and when they reached the sacred stone they would be formally presented to the crowd and asked to swear allegiance to the Council by each in turn raising their right hand and swearing the oath.

'Zalta, zalta, zalta. I swear my allegiance to the Council of Maritania.'

Abi had reluctantly agreed to the ceremony after having at first been very opposed to getting involved in what she called hocus pocus, myth and magic. She had explained her reservations to Isla saying that she didn't think it was right for her to sign up to something she didn't believe in.

Isla understood her worry but pointed out that she was in a different world now and should make judgements based on present circumstances, like they were all having to do. She said that Abi was now living amongst people who had all sworn allegiance and that meant they had sworn to help each other to survive their ordeal in Maritania. She then reminded Abi that she also had some responsibility as the eldest, for the safety of her younger brother and sister who would no doubt follow her lead, so she should consider her decision wisely. Knowing that Isla would always speak with her heart and give wise council Abi didn't have to think about it for too long.

Having left their coats, scarves and hats in the boat at the moorings, it was a little chilly outside at nights so Isla had made each of them a simple wrap around cloak to keep the cold off during the ceremony. The long procession made its way out of the camp in a direction they hadn't been before. As they walked along behind Will, Isla and Nico, despite the cape, Zach could hear Abi give the odd shiver.

'You alright Abi?' Zach said as he leaned in a little closer to her.

'Just a little cold,' she said through chattering teeth. 'I think I might be going down with something.'

'Here,' said Zach as he pulled his bobble hat from his pocket and handed it to her. 'That'll warm you up.'

Abi took it and pulled it over her head, grateful for its comfort.

'Fly Canaries fly,' she whispered, and gave him a cheeky grin.

They walked on for another ten minutes or so, the sound of the howling of wolves in the distance floating across the still night air. Abi glanced over to her right, and high up on the furthest horizon saw what she could only imagine was the Mountain of Dreams with the fullest of full moons shining brightly above it. She also fancied she saw, silhouetted across the moon, the outline of a big, black, howling wolf.

As they moved on they began to hear the regular beat of a drum that got louder and louder as they approached a large, open area with a gigantic stone in the middle of it. Beside the stone was a wooden platform where the other members of the Council were stood. When they reached the central stone, the crowds peeled off to the right and left and stood in a large circle facing inwards towards the platform. This left Isla, Nico and Will in front of the brightly lit platform with Izzie, who was holding Millie's lead, Zach and Abi close in behind them. When all were in place, the drum stopped beating and the Facilitator, Professor Fitzjohn, stepped forward.

'Tonight being the Wolf Moon, the first Lunatum since the arrival of our new brethren, we gather to welcome them and hear them swear allegiance to the

Council of Maritania and by so doing, allegiance to us all. Firstly our sister Isabella.' Isla ushered Izzie round onto the platform.

'Raise your right hand and repeat after me,' said the Facilitator.

'Zalta, zalta, zalta, I, Isabella Storm pledge allegiance to the Council of Maritania.'

Izzie did as she was told and after a round of applause went back to her place behind Isla. Next up was Zach and he went through the same procedure pledging his allegiance in the same manner. Then it was Abi's turn and as she stepped forward from behind Will out into the light of the platform, there was a huge gasp from the crowd. Some began wailing and the Council members all reeled back in shock and surprise and The Facilitator raised both hands in the air.

'Elora, Elora, Elora,' he cried out in a loud, alarmed voice. The crowd immediately joined in, some falling to their knees and bowing their heads as they did so.

Not knowing what to think, Abi looked frightened. Seeing her in distress, Will stepped forward and went down on one knee before her.

'Fear not Abigail Storm. All is well and all will be well. We have waited a long time for your arrival so you must forgive our exaltations and be patient as all will become known to you.'

As he said this he stood up and held out his arm for her to take and then he walked her over the platform towards the large stone in the centre. As they got closer

Abi could see the outline of a figure carved in the stone with the name Elora above it. Closer still and she could make out the general outline of someone in a cape just as she was dressed. Finally she began to make out girlish features with shoulder-length, straight hair flowing down from underneath a band, carved around the figure's forehead. It was then that she realised why she was the centre of attention. There, around the band, was a series of birds identical to the canaries on Zach's bobble hat.

'No, no,' she cried. 'It's not me, it's Zach.' Will looked at her with sympathetic eyes.

'We have waited many years. We know the Elora's features well. The eyes are your eyes, and the lips and hair are yours, not Zach's,' said Will.

'But the band around my head is Zach's,' Abi pleaded. 'It is his hat with the birds on it, not mine.'

'That may be Abi, but it is clearly written in the Priscus Percepta that on arrival the Elora will appear just as on the stone. It matters not whose band of birds it is, all that matters is the person that arrives wearing it. You are the Elora, not Zach. That is how it is written. None of us know as yet how, but somehow, you will lead us back to where we belong, out of Maritania and back to our homes. It may take time and you may not know how it will come about, but the prophecy was foretold by the elders long ago and the first part of that prophecy has come true with your arrival.'

Just as he finished speaking Isla came across to them

and held out her hand to Abi.

'Come brave heart, be strong, take my hand and swear allegiance to the Council of Maritania as Izzie and Zach have done. Whenever we can, we will help and support you in your quest, just as you will help us, but you must start by swearing allegiance as it is written.'

With that Abi went back with Isla and swore allegiance like Zach and Izzie. The crowd then cheered and clapped. The drum started up again and Abi, Zach and Izzie with Will, Isla, Nico and the Council started off back to the camp. The torchlit crowd followed on behind chanting, 'Elora, Elora' all the way.

That night Abi tossed and turned, unable to sleep with everything buzzing in her head. As she lay there she could hear Isla moving about in the next room and got up and went to see what she was doing so late into the night.

As she entered the main living area Isla was stood by the table with the hilt of her broadsword in one hand as she used a damp rag to wipe the blade down with the other. Her leather shield lay face down on the table exposing the inner straps that bound it to Isla's left arm. Her strong left arm that parried the blows in the heat of battle. Isla had a faraway look in her eye and was so absorbed in lovingly caring for her trusty sword, and no doubt reminiscing about her past exploits with her kinsmen, that she didn't notice Abi entering.

'Ahmm,' Abi gave a little cough. 'Do you mind if I sit awhile? I can't sleep.'

'Come, come my bonnie lass, your head must be spinning. Come sit and rest. Your burden must lie heavy on such young shoulders. We all have challenges to face in life, be they large or small it matters not. It is how we face those challenges that counts and not just whether we win or lose. The biggest lessons in life are most often learned from when we fail, so fear of failure must never put us off trying. Not to try would be the real failure and I believe you have the spirit to give your heart and soul to the task, no matter the consequences.'

'Oh Isla, I wish to be brave like you. It feels like the hopes of everyone in Maritania to get back to their loved ones, lie in my hands and I have no idea what I am supposed to do.'

'You must trust in yourself little one. You and Zach and Izzie are unique here. It is not your choice to have come here without being summoned and it was not your choice to be the Elora. It was decided by the elders and written in the Priscus Percepta many years ago. You must not take yourself to task, you must believe and all will be well.'

Abi sat with her eyes closed quietly contemplating for a moment or two what Isla had said. Then, having taken it on board, instead of expressing her worries and doubts she asked her first positive question.

'Isla, I remember you telling us about you being in the King's cavalry and losing a great battle at Dunbar where you were heavily defeated by Cromwell. Having fought in battles and won and lost, what do you think makes the difference between winning and losing, success and failure, victory and defeat?'

'Well Abi, I don't know if they are the most critical aspects in battle, or indeed in life, but a good start is to prepare well by learning all you can about the capabilities of your opponent and the geography of the battleground. Most of all, make allies out of those who might otherwise become your enemies.'

This last statement pulled Abi up with a start.

'What do you mean make allies out of those who might become my enemies?'

'Well Abi. Think back to the Council meeting. If anyone there was to become your enemy, who do you think it would be most likely to be?'

'Well, Roseanna I suppose. She pulled me up on everything I said and even accused me and Zach and Izzie of being spies sent into the camp by the Summoner.'

'So, where would you rather have Roseanna?' Isla said with questioning eyes.

'Oh I see what you mean,' said Abi. 'She could make a dangerous enemy if I were to ignore her. On the other hand if I were to show her respect and keep her close by my side, she might become a very trustworthy and loyal ally.' Abi closed her eyes again and recalled times in her own short life when she could have at least held out a hand to those she wasn't sure of, but didn't and then regretted it. She made a mental note not to rush to judgement on people who might have had other intentions but didn't express themselves very well. She also accepted however that she was still young and inexperienced, so she should not be too hard on herself.

'Wise words Isla. I have much to learn and must learn it quickly.'

'Don't punish yourself child. I say again your destiny was chosen for you and you can only do as your heart dictates. Always remember that just as you have been chosen as the Elora, so others, including those who have waited patiently to welcome you, will be with you in every way.'

Isla's words brought solace to Abi's soul and she felt much more content and positive than she had just a few moments ago. She excused herself, thanked Isla again for her wise words and went back to bed to rest. As she lay quietly in the still, dark night she fancied she heard in the far distance the plaintive, lonesome howls of the big black wolf, which seemed to be calling out to her like a long lost soul.

~ CHAPTER THIRTEEN ~

Escape from Maritania

Abi rose early and sought out Isla, Will and Nico to ask if it was possible to arrange a Council meeting. They assured her that as the Elora, the Council was at her service and went off to make arrangements with the Facilitator and the other Council members for a meeting in an hour's time.

Abi then went to find Izzie and Zach to explain to them that, even though she didn't think she was the Elora, others clearly thought she was and she would try her best to help them.

'To you though, I am the same Abi, the same sister that I have always been and will always be.'

'Oh come on Abi. You know us better than that. We have always been there for each other and always will be,' said Zach.

'Sorry,' said Abi with a tearful look in her eye which surprised them both. 'I just didn't want you to think I had really changed when I carry out the duties of the Elora. That would break my heart.' Izzie got up and went over to her and gave her a hug and whispered something in her ear.

'Thanks Izzie, you funny little thing. Love you forever always too,' Abi said as she dabbed her eyes with her handkerchief and gave Izzie a tearful smile. Millie also seemed to sense Abi's awkwardness and went over, sat down in front of her and offered her paw.

'Ah Millie,' Abi smiled down at her. 'I haven't forgotten you.' She bent down, scooped her up and gave her a big hug as Millie licked at her face.

'Whatever you need to do and whatever has to be done, we will be there for you no matter what,' said Zach. 'Don't ever think on it again.'

Abi arrived at the Council chamber to find that an extra chair had been provided at the table and that the professor had vacated his seat and gestured to Abi that she should take his place in the chair of the Facilitator. They all stood up and then sat down again only when Abi had sat down.

The Priscus Percepta and the sacred paddle lay on the table immediately in front of her. Abi decided to ignore them and see if her position as Elora would allow her to make changes to procedures without any dissent. After all, she thought to herself, what was the point in waiting for the Elora and then just carrying on as before.

She had made compromises to her principles in order to protect her younger siblings. Surely the Council would be willing to make similar compromises to help her find a way out of Maritania as was foretold. She wasn't sure how far her powers went and wanted to test them out to see how the Council would react.

'Members of the Council,' she said. Immediately there was a tension in the room as they looked first at Abi and then at the Priscus Percepta and the paddle and then back to Abi. The professor looked alarmed that procedures weren't being followed and opened his mouth to say something but then thought better of it.

'Now that I have sworn allegiance and been accepted by all as the Elora I first of all want to ask for your support and understanding. It is written that I will lead you out of Maritania but it does not show the path we need to take to do so. I therefore ask for your patience as I try to unravel the mystery of Maritania and my part within it.

'What is clear to me is that Zach, Izzie and myself are unsummoned, unlike anyone else here. This hopefully signifies that Aquavena has less power over us and maybe I, as the Elora, can have access to ways forward that you have not had available to you. Don't be surprised therefore if I choose pathways that are unfamiliar to you.

'When I first arrived in Maritania I thought it strange that you had not made any attempt to overcome the scrones and make your way back to where you have all come from. I now understand that any such battle would have been fruitless and dangerous because what would be the point of the risk, when even if you were successful, you didn't know the way out.

'Your belief from the Priscus Percepta was that you had to wait for the Elora and you have done so and now I am here. It would seem that so far everything is unfolding as it was written. This being so, I am not as doubting as I once was. However, there is nothing written about how the Elora will lead you out of Maritania, only that she will. Again I ask for your patience.

'What has already become clear to me is that you all have been summoned for offences against Aquavena's waters. What strikes me most of all about that, is it would appear Aquavena is punishing those who carry out the offences rather than those who are actually responsible for them.

'Take Isla and Nico who were forced at the point of a sword to help drain the fens by those who threw the locals off their fishing grounds and changed it to farmland to increase profits for themselves and become rich at others expense. It is the same the world over. No doubt all of you have similar stories to tell, tricked by those who wish to exploit the people and the land and seas for their own gain. It is not you who are destroying Aquavena's oceans seas, lakes and rivers. You are merely pawns in the hands of those with power who seek more and more for themselves, whatever the cost to our world.

'In many places, the waters of the world are polluted for profit, the sea-beds wrecked for profit, the fishing stocks plundered for profit, waste fills the oceans and seas, cruelly destroying Aquavena's kingdom for profit. We mustn't play their game. No more destruction and pollution of the Earth's resources to fill the purses of the privileged and powerful. No more.'

To Abi's delight, the first of them to respond, and this time with not a thought for the paddle, was Roseanna.

'How do we know you are not one of those who would lie to us and deceive us? How do we know you are not lying to us and deceiving us now?'

'Wise words Roseanna,' Abi replied with Isla's advice ringing in her ears. 'I would only ask you look into your own heart to find the truth. When I look into mine I see that you are an honest and trustworthy soul who wishes only to do your best for all of us. You have waited a long time for salvation? Ask yourself, what have you got to lose? I say throw off the shackles that tie you down and follow your heart. You are a young, strong, powerful woman with a free spirit. I ask that you resolve to break down any of the superstitions that hold us back and help us by playing a major part in our battle.'

'Of what battle do you speak Elora?' replied Roseanna.

'Why the battle to free our minds and hearts from

the tyranny that surrounds us. The battle you must embrace with all your heart and soul to seize victory from the depths of despair and release us from this imposed exile here in Maritania.

'Aquavena has condemned you unjustly and built this land around you to keep you away from her waters. We must remove the barriers to your freedom one by one before we can finally discover the pathway to Aquavena herself and confront the injustice you all face. Only when we have understood and overcome the known obstacles – the castle, the, scrones and their support network through the cave to the Leviathan, can we then concern ourselves with the unknown mysteries surrounding Aquavena. Abi looked around the room and then spoke to the whole Council the words they had been waiting to hear.

'Even though I must admit I did not believe that I was the Elora, I understand what is expected of me by those who believe otherwise and I cannot let them down. Their expectation is great and I call on all of you to help me fulfil their desires and return them and all of us to our rightful time and place as soon as we can. What say you? Are we one?'

There was no taking a vote, no paddles, no hand on the Priscus Percepta and no hesitancy from anyone as they all responded as one voice.

'We are one.'

'Good,' said Abi. 'I will outline the plan and we will carry it out when you all agree we are ready to proceed.

Some preparations will be required. The first of these is that I must survey the land to see what strategies might best suit any battle plans. In the meantime, ready the horses and stoke up the armoury with as many weapons as we can muster. I will ride out today with Will, Isla, Nico and Roseanna, to gain their knowledge and advice on what may or may not be the best way forward. Zach, Izzie and Millie must come too as I would as always feel lost without them. We shall have another meeting of the Council tomorrow to agree the way forward and finalise preparations. Does anyone have anything else they wish to discuss?'

'Erm.' Professor Fitzjohn tentatively raised his hand. It felt especially strange for him having his hand in the air without the paddle in it or without his other hand on the Priscus Percepta.

'I don't know if this is appropriate but should I dispense with the Facilitator's headwear and robe, now that I am no longer the Facilitator?'

'You may wear what you wish, like everyone else Professor. If that is what you feel comfortable wearing, now that we are all aware that they are not symbols of authority any more, then by all means wear them.'

'Thank you Elora. I will still wear them if I may. I was made Facilitator a long time ago and have grown comfortable in them.'

'Who made you Facilitator?' asked Abi.

'I was elected by the Council,' replied the professor.

'Who was on the Council at the time?' The

professor paused for a second or two, clasped his hands together in his lap and with a bowed head, stared down at them as if he was concentrating very hard.

'Many have come and gone since then Elora, I'm not sure,' he said in a far off way as if he was still trying hard to remember. 'No, I'm sorry, I am at a loss, I really can't remember.' Abi was a little surprised that he couldn't remember those who had voted him into office.

~ CHAPTER FOURTEEN ~

The Leviathan

That afternoon the horses were readied and mounted up, forming a loose posse with Will taking the lead. He had roamed Maritania almost every day in his search for Polly and knew the lie of the land better than anyone else. Behind him came Abi, Izzie and Zach. Zach's horse was also carrying Millie who seemed to enjoy seeing the world from a whole different viewpoint. Behind them came Roseanna and Isla, with Nico bringing up the rear.

They moved through the camp saluting anyone they came across with the 'zalta' greeting. Some they met realised that Abi was one of those greeting them and bowed and called out to her,

'God bless you Elora. God be with you.' Abi, true to her word to the Council, acknowledged their cries and blessings without any hint of discomfort or denial.

'Zalta, we are one,' she smiled back at them.

Will led them out of the camp at the far end, the same as he had done with Zach. Just as before, it was like stepping into another world. The cries of the gulls and the sound of the waves breaking and surging up the beach filled Abi and Izzie with pure joy. The sight of the majestic galleon, the Leviathan, resting on the ocean with its figurehead in the shape of a giant sea monster, took their breath away. Abi dismounted and invited Izzie to do the same. She then told the others to wait there as she and Izzie walked slowly, side by side, down the beach to the shoreline.

Once there, they both stood stock still looking straight ahead out over the ocean, their jet black hair buffeting in the sea breeze.

'Well what do you think Izzie?' said Abi, as she swept her hair out of her face, squinted her eyes a little and stared out to sea at the Leviathan.

'Reckon we could make it?'

Izzie was silent for a moment.

'Reckon we could Abi, and back again,' she smiled.

Abi cast her eye across the whole sweep of the bay until it finally rested on the headland off to the right, nearest to where the Leviathan lay at anchor. She could see the cave entrance below the rocky outcrop of the headland. Her eye then followed the outline of the landscape back inland as it slowly descended to what looked like a grassy plain sweeping around the far side of the camp. Having travelled to the camp from the castle on the day that they escaped, she estimated that the grassy area would stretch round somewhere near to where the castle was.

They turned and walked back up the beach to where Will was holding their horses for them. As soon as she got there, Abi turned to Will.

'If you follow that headland down to the grassy plain below, does that then go around the camp and all the way to the castle?'

'Yes,' said Will. 'It's about three miles or so that way. It is mainly open country but there are a few spinneys of trees dotted here and there that you would have to go around.'

'And what's on the other side of that headland beyond the cave?' asked Abi.

'The sea comes in to an isolated cove but it's really difficult to get down there from the clifftop so it's pretty much deserted.'

Abi thanked him and she and Izzie remounted and they all headed off to take a closer look. They soon reached the wide open expanse of grass and could see further inland where it narrowed in towards the tree spinneys as Will had said. Abi indicated to Will to go a little further so she could see through the trees and beyond. On the other side of them it opened out again and in the far distance she could make out the very top of the castle battlements and Aquavena's flag fluttering in the breeze.

Having surveyed the land, Abi turned them around to retrace their steps back to the bay and the beach. As they trotted slowly back, she felt a presence coming up from behind on her right-hand side. Abi, half-turning round, was a little surprised to see Roseanna leaning over towards her.

'Forgive me Elora but can I speak with you.' She indicated with her eyes that she meant privately, further back behind the others. Abi nodded and stood still as she waited for the rest to ride on until she and Roseanna were out of earshot. As they went by, she simply told them that they would follow on.

'What is it Roseanna?' Abi asked.

'I just want you to know that my history is one where I have in the past been betrayed by those close to me. That makes me nervous and suspicious of those around me. With that in mind, I hope you will forgive me for my outbursts against you in the Council. I did not know you were the Elora and now that I do, I want you to know that my heart and my soul will be with you in every way.

'Having said that, I do believe that someone on the Council has been betraying us since long before you came. Will has made several plans to breech the castle to see if he can find Polly inside, but each time he does, they seem to be waiting for him and he is forced to flee. Jago also had a plan to take a crew over the headland, scale the cliffs, and steal their supply boat so that they could row out to sea in search of a way out of Maritania.

Again, they were waiting for him, and he and the others were lucky to escape with their lives. I just wish to warn you to be careful who you give your confidences to.'

Abi rode along silently for a minute or so, quietly contemplating Roseanna's suspicions. Then she put a hand out on Roseanna's shoulder.

'As you ask for forgiveness, so do I Roseanna. I was quick to condemn you without just cause and my hope is that as Izzie is my sister, you and I will be sisters in word and deed. I admire your spirit and I am sure your loyalty and stalwart heart will be of great service to us all.'

With that, they exchanged a quick, silent zalta sign and Abi trotted off back to take up her place just behind Will. They had by now returned to the beach, and with a last glance at the headland, the ship and the ocean, they wheeled their horses to the left to follow Will as he took the same path he had taken with Zach, a day or so earlier.

They were soon passing the high rocks and the stream and the dense woods the wolf had appeared from. Abi was looking for somewhere they might surprise the enemy and lure them into a trap. At several places amongst the rocks they stopped and discussed various options but nothing seemed to present itself as an obvious place to carry out such a plan. In any case, she thought to herself, why would the castle soldiers come out to chase us if we were heading away from the castle. Maybe, if we had stolen something from them that they had to get back, like the Summoner for instance. Capture him and we may just stand a chance. For the moment, she kept that idea to herself.

As they were riding out of the rocky area into the open, Will turned in his saddle and pointed over into the far distance. Abi cast her eyes in the direction he was pointing and was shocked to see the size of the massive mountain that towered high into the sky on the distant horizon.

'The Mountain of Dreams,' he said. 'Once seen never forgotten.' Zach again pictured the mighty flock of eagles with the huge fish in their talons flying overhead as Abi and Izzie just stared spellbound. It was Zach who broke the silence.

'You know I told you Abi that as you go towards it the mountain disappears, well I just wonder if that is also true for you as the Elora. Maybe the Elora is the only one who can break that spell and reach the mountain?'

So many unexplainable events had happened to Abi that she was reluctant to dabble in testing out even more myth and magic. Understanding their urgent need to find a way home however, she agreed it might be worth a try. She asked the others to wait there for her.

Alone, she followed the winding path into the distance towards the mountain. She set off at a gentle trot and before long broke into a canter. The others watched her progress and could see the dust fly up around her horse's feet so that she looked to them to be floating towards the mountain on a magical cloud. She continued on for a good distance and then the cloud slowed and stopped. They could see it moving this way and that as if she was searching for something and then they saw the cloud coming back towards them.

'Why did you turn back Abi?' Izzie urgently asked on her return.

'I turned back when the Mountain of Dreams suddenly disappeared as you said it would.'

'No, no,' said Izzie. 'It didn't disappear. Honest Abi.' Abi looked around at the others and their nods of agreement made it clear that they, like Izzie, didn't see it disappear.

'It is a mystery indeed, for it got smaller as I got closer and then disappeared altogether. Most strange, but enough for now. Will, lead on and show us any other routes to the castle and anything you think might be helpful or otherwise.'

Will wheeled his horse around and led them out of the rocks into a wide, green plain with only the odd bush here and there. Off to their right was a vast landscape with a mixture of woods and open areas that went on as far as the eye could see, finally ending in some rolling hills against the horizon. Will explained to Abi that he had roamed those lands over and over in search of Polly. In doing so, he had found nothing of any note there and in any case there was no other way to the castle in that direction.

They turned a little to the left and then, all together, side by side rather than one behind the other, they trotted down the open plain for a mile or two. There they came to a point where there were very steep, rocky outcrops on either side of them. They loomed above a shallow, but fast flowing river, with a stony bed and the odd larger rock breaking out above the surface. It was a river like nothing you would normally see in the fen.

'It is very much like Alban here,' said Isla as they dismounted to give the horses a rest and a chance to drink at one of the slower running pools along the edge.

'Every time I come here I fancy I can hear the ghosts of my fathers as the river speaks to me and calls me home.' As she said that something caught her eye. Looking up she saw a large eagle soaring effortlessly around the top of the highest peak.

The scenery reminded Izzie of Isla's story except it was even more beautiful than she could have imagined.

'I would love to visit the land of the Alban,' she said.

'I'm sure you will one day,' said Nico, in soft low tones as he heaved himself up and remounted his horse. 'The Elora has come and we must believe, and all will be well.'

They crossed the sparkling waters and carried on down the grassy plain for a mile or so. As they rounded a bend, in the far distance, the castle came into view. The way ahead led right up to the moat and the battlements beyond. Immediately, Abi noticed that once again the castle looked much smaller from a distance but grew larger as they approached it.

As this was happening, it struck Abi that the enlargement of the castle as you got closer was as puzzling as the disappearance of the Mountain of

Dreams as you got closer. She made a mental note to herself that maybe there is some sort of visual distortion or optical illusion going on and therefore it was possible that other aspects of Maritania might not be quite what they seem.

Will and Abi halted for a brief discussion about what they had seen so far, and then Will headed them all back to camp by a shortcut through the trees.

That night Abi lay awake running through her mind everything she had seen and heard that day. What would be the best way to attack the castle? What size and type of opposition were they likely to face from the scrones? Was Roseanna correct in her belief that someone on the Council was a traitor? If she was correct, who was it and should she use that information to set a false trail?

Her place as the Elora was weighing heavily on her shoulders. Despite the fact that she continually told herself that she did not actually believe that she was the Elora, she was very aware that her decisions could be critical to her younger brother and sister. That fact alone caused her great worry and concern. Eventually, more from exhaustion than any comfort or satisfaction from having worked out a way forward, she drifted off.

~ CHAPTER FIFTEEN ~

The Crown of Elora

Abi awoke the next morning to find that her mind had been working hard through the night. The way forward now seemed much less confusing to her than it had done before she had fallen asleep. The battle ahead would be a battle of the mind as much as a physical battle. Indeed it was quite plain to her that the last thing they should do was cause great harm to Aquavena's creatures so that she would be angered and never release them from Maritania. They must do their best to drive the scrones out of their lairs in order that they can clear a path to finding Aquavena and, through her, a way back home.

To Abi, it had resolved itself into what amounted to a three-pronged assault. A head-on attack to drive them out of the castle via the underground cave. Next, the blocking of the cave entrance behind them so they could not return that way, and finally capturing the Leviathan so that they would have no refuge and nowhere to go but out to sea and away. There was little time to lose. Abi once again called a Council meeting for early that day so as to give them as much time as possible to agree and finalise battle plans and prepare for the fray.

As Abi entered the Council chamber, Zach and Izzie went to take up their seats on the far side of the room where they had sat, along with Millie, on all previous occasions. At the same time, all of the Council stood up but Abi quickly ushered them down again.

'Please, please, we are one.' She then took her seat and looked around the room at each of them one by one.

'As you all know, it is said that I, the Elora, will come and lead you out of the land of Maritania and back to your own world in your own place and time. To that end I will do everything I can to fulfil that prophecy. However, I want you all to know that should at any point I fall in battle, then you must carry on without me. The prophecy does not say that I will come with you, it only says that my coming will lead you on to the right path. So, should I not be with you, you must continue on, and find your own way home from there.' She gave the zalta salute. 'We are one,' she said.

'We are one,' they repeated with nods of agreement and understanding.

'To matters of business,' said Abi.

'They are many and we are few. However the

scrones are as much prisoners here as we are. This is not their proper home and they are probably also not happy away from their families and loved ones and their natural place in the world. This gives us the advantage in that we are fighting for our lives and freedom whereas they are only fighting to remain here as prison guards and servants to Aquavena.

'That being the case, I propose to start with a surprise attack on the castle. If they are not expecting it, we can breech the walls and get inside and then drive them out down the underground tunnel and back to the sea by the cave entrance. Roseanna, Isla, myself and Izzie will lead the charge and carry out the assault on the castle.

'In the meantime Will, Zach, Nico and Jago once we have driven them out, we need you to block the cave entrance back into the castle so that they can't return there easily from the sea. There are rocky outcrops above the cave so as soon as the scrones have run out, do your best to send as many rocks tumbling down to block the entrance. Even if it doesn't cut them off completely it will at least slow down any attempted return by that route. Are we all clear?' asked Abi.

'Well yes dear. It all seemed very clear to me and Lucille,' Loretta said as she looked towards Lucille for approval.

'Just one thing dear,' she continued a little hesitantly. 'What about our role. What part shall Lucille and I be taking in the battle?'

Lucille looked at her sharply with an expression which showed some surprise at the suggestion that either she or Loretta would be of any use in armed combat.

'The most important role of all,' said Abi. 'You will be our field hospital. You will follow on behind with the necessary supplies of water and dressings to treat the wounded and bring cheer and comfort to those who have fallen. I will supply you both with a horse and cart and a driver to follow us into battle.'

'Excuse me dear, begging your pardon, but you will do no such thing. In our younger days, Lucille and I used to race horse-drawn buggies up and down the embassy driveway. Even the sergeant-at-arms couldn't keep up with us. You need every hand you can muster, we will be quite happy to drive the first aid carts ourselves.'

'I thank you both, so be it,' said Abi.

'Professor Fitzjohn. Would you assist the ladies with the first aid? I fear they made need help to get some of the heavier of our wounded up into the carts.'

'Certainly,' said Professor Fitzjohn. I will be happy to assist in any way I can.'

Abi was about to end the meeting when Will stood up, and slightly bowing his head he turned to face her.

'Elora. We wish to make some presentations to you, Zach and Izzie in readiness for our quest. May we?'

Abi looked a little puzzled but knowing Will so well she had no hesitation in granting his request. With that Will nodded to Isla who rose and went out of the room followed by Nico, Roseanna and then Will himself.

First to return was Isla followed by Nico and Will. Each carried a fabulously ornate, silver-hilted sword and scabbard, hung from a leather belt. As they entered the others all stood up. Isla stopped in front of Izzie while Nico lined up in front of Zach and Will in front of Abi. They each bowed and presented the swords. Abi, Zach and Izzie each took their sword, strapped it around their waist and bowed in recognition and thanks for the wonderful quality and craftsmanship of the gifts.

Will indicated to Zach and Izzie that they should step back a little. Then Roseanna entered the room, this time with a red, velvet cushion with a golden crown on it. She moved with some speed and purpose towards Abi and all in one movement went down on one knee before her, bowed her head, raised the cushion and with great reverence said only one word.

'Elora.'

There on the cushion sat the most beautifully fashioned golden crown. It had a ring of canaries impressed into it all around the headpiece, just like the band on the head of the Elora on the stone plaque. On either side of the crown a pair of wings rose up a little from the decorated headband and then folded back along either side.

Will stepped forward, lifted the crown from the cushion and placed it on her head. He then took one step back and bowed sharply.

'All hail Elora, all hail,' he said.

The others, including this time Zach and Izzie,

caught up in the moment, followed suit.

'All hail Elora, all hail.'

With that the twins suddenly remembered that they too had gifts, this time for the Elora and Izzie. They left the room and very soon returned and with a small curtsey, presented each of them in turn with a neatly folded bundle.

Izzie's consisted of a royal blue cover with frilled, silver trim for her horse and a matching tunic and breeches in the same blue with silver edgings. Abi received the same but her cover and clothing were in red with gold trim. The quality of the sewing was exquisite in every detail with the silver for Izzie matching her mainly silver-coloured, piebald. Abi's was red and gold, to show off the handsome physique of her grand, black stallion and reflect the red and gold clothing of royal patronage. Abi and Izzie thanked them both and the twins seemed to enjoy enormously this brief reminder of the pomp and ceremony that they had been used to in previous times.

With that Abi thanked them all once again for their gifts and said that she would speak with each of them individually to discuss any details they needed more guidance on, or anything further they felt they needed to bring to her attention.

Later that evening Abi went alone to see Nico and Jago. She apologised if she had misled them at the Council meeting. She had concerns that someone on the Council might be betraying them and had a strong suspicion who that might be. She wanted to use this to their advantage by laying a false trail to give them some advantage on the day.

'Who do you suspect Elora,' said Nico.

'I must keep my confidences and trust in my decisions. It will do no-one any good if I speak out of turn and I am proved to be wrong.' She then explained to them her real plan for their part in the battle.

'Once we have driven the scrones out of the castle, instead of helping Will and Zach, I would like you take a dozen men and clamber down the cliffs on the far side of the headland and come round from behind to surprise them. If you can take the boat, you can row out to the Leviathan whilst she is least defended and see what you can do to disable or disarm her.

Both Nico and Jago assured her they understood and that they would keep her words to themselves.

~ CHAPTER SIXTEEN ~

The Battle: Part One

The day had arrived. There was a fresh breeze that rustled the leaves on the trees and unsettled the horses in the paddock. Flecks of pure white cloud scudded across a sunny, bright blue sky and even the humblest of creatures in the wood seemed unusually quiet with anticipation. The bees, that on any ordinary day would tirelessly buzz from flower to flower, bending the lip and clambering inside into their own secret world, were today silent and still. The absence of the singing of the birds that normally heralded the dawning of a new day, gave the sense that today was not just any other day. Today history was in the making.

Abi had risen early and taken herself off to her quiet space behind the paddock, where she stood in deep contemplation. She was telling herself that she had done everything she could in preparation for what was to come. She was working her mind into a state of positivity so that she would not transmit or betray any hint of nervousness or worry among those who had put their faith in her.

For a fleeting moment, she did wonder why a test like this should come to her when she was so young. She soon dismissed this thought when she remembered Isla's words about each of us having our own destiny to fulfil, no matter how or when the challenges might arise.

The night before, Abi had sent out final orders through Will, Isla, Nico, Jago and Roseanna and already everyone was busy checking their weapons and preparing the horses. There was the clang of hammers on metal as swords were finally tempered and spear points sharpened. You could hear the jingle of the bridles and stirrups and the odd whinnying of a young colt or filly, seeming to smell a little fear in the air. Alternatively, some of the fully grown stallions and mares tore and stamped at the ground in anticipation, anxious for the trial and the glory of the momentous day to begin.

The sight, sound and smell of the horses being readied, took Will back to the St Winnold's day horse fair and inevitably to thoughts of Polly. He fancied it was Polly he could see standing by a large black stallion at the back of the paddock grooming its sides till its flanks shone, showing off the rippling muscles in its powerful haunches. He couldn't take his eyes off of her until just as he was about to cry out 'Polly, Polly,' she turned a little to talk to a man beside her who was fitting the bridle on his horse, and Will could see instantly that it wasn't her. It was a cruel trick of the light for him to be cheated again but it only made him more determined that one day he would find her.

They were upwards of one hundred and fifty horses in all and Abi, in consultation with Isla and Roseanna, who had both fought battles on horseback before, had split them into three separate fighting forces. Abi had been advised by them that they would be more flexible and able to react quicker and better to circumstances as three smaller units rather than one large one.

That being the case, Roseanna was to lead the left flank, Isla the right flank, with Abi in charge of the centre ground and overall command. She was in overall command because she was the Elora but, she made it quite clear to Roseanna and Isla that they were to make decisions as they saw fit on the day and did not need her permission.

Abi had chosen to ride the same black stallion she had done the other day. It was a mightily impressive beast and would greatly inspire confidence in the army behind her. She threw the red and gold cloth over him, buckled on her sword and mounted her horse. Izzie handed up the crown of Elora, which fitted Abi perfectly, and gave her the look of a queen leading her troops into battle.

Izzie, similarly spread her blue cloth with silver

trim, over her smaller, more nimble piebald. She then strapped the belt and sword around her waist and was soon up astride her horse. Isla passed up the flag that Izzie was to carry into battle. It was the Royalist flag from Isla's wall, but as Isla pointed out, in battle, almost any flag is better than no flag. She also explained to Izzie that the flag should always be at the front of the centre ground so that all the army could see it and follow it. Therefore it was better, because of her position on the battlefield, that Izzie was the standard bearer. Isla also told her how important it was that she kept the flag flying.

'Your army will follow the flag to the last. Keep it aloft at all times and we shall be victorious.' These were the words ringing in Izzie's ears as she finally readied herself for this momentous day.

Following the plan she had outlined the previous night, Will and Zach, with Millie beside him, had already started making their way to the bottom of the headland where they would tie up their horses and proceed on foot up to the very top of the cliff above the entrance to the cave that led into and out of the castle. They took with them axes to chop large branches off of the trees. They intended to use them as levers to cause a landslide and hopefully block the cave entrance below.

At the same time Nico and Jago had left along with Will and Zach to meet outside the camp with a dozen others and then clamber over the headland and down the far side onto the deserted beach. There they would wait in readiness to steal the scrones boat and carry out a surprise attack on the Leviathan if the opportunity arose.

Back at the camp, Abi gave the signal to mount up. They then began to make their way to the high peaks on the castle side of the fast flowing, stony river. There they would take up their positions on the grassy plain, ready for the attack. Abi led the way with Izzie behind as they slowly rode through the woods on the path that Will had shown them. It led them straight to the river.

Abi rode out to the centre of the open ground and her battalion lined up behind her. Next came Isla who, as she rode along in front of Abi and Izzie to take up the right flank, bowed her head slightly and then kissed the ring on her finger and reached out to touch her flag. As she did so a smile broke out on her face.

'Long live this day,' she rang out with her very heart and soul. 'Victory will be ours.'

Her troops lined up behind her and finally Roseanna took up the left flank with her battalion. When all was settled Abi rode out in front. As she did so, her horse spun in circles and reared up a little with excitement and anticipation. Abi pulled on the reins and settled it down until it stood quietly under her control.

'Citizens of Maritania and of the Kingdoms of all the Earth, our mission this day is not to take the lives of those who stand against us but to drive them out so that we might take back our freedom. Our freedom to live as we would wish to live, whilst respecting the needs and rights of all living things who share our home.

'We must throw off the shackles of this imprisonment and expose the real enemies of Aquavena. Those who would sell their neighbours for rich profits, those who would plunder the land and the sea to line their own pockets, those who lie and cheat and buy their way to power by the betrayal of the people. Greed and deceit shall never triumph. It only exists in the minds of those who have sold their souls and lost their faith in common humanity and force their twisted versions of the truth upon us.

'Be merciful with our enemies for they are merely pawns in a war fashioned by others. Follow your hearts, let the beautiful face of justice shine down upon you and victory will be ours.'

With that she raised her sword in the air, turned her horse around and began to slowly advance towards the castle. The line followed behind her crying 'Elora. Elora,' swords drawn.

Behind them came two horse-drawn carts laden with makeshift medical supplies to treat the injured. At the reins were Loretta on one and Lucille on the other. They had waited as long as they could but Professor Fitzjohn didn't arrive. The twins were not convinced that he would have the stomach for the fight and weren't too surprised when he failed to show up.

As usual they were rather overdressed for the occasion. They smiled heartily at each other recalling, no doubt, when they were little girls and used to mimic their father's guards out on parade, marching up and down the drawing room with fire pokers for swords.

The line moved forward slowly with the centre a little ahead of the flanks. When they turned the bend which brought the castle into view, Abi saw at once that, just as Roseanna had feared, they had been betrayed.

Outside the castle was a line of at least two hundred mounted troops in full armour with swords and lances at the ready. Abi raised her hand and her cavalry stopped behind her. There was about half a mile between the two armies and they eyed each other cautiously. Then Abi turned directly towards them, raised her sword high in the air and gave a final rallying cry to her troops.

'Be not afraid, we are one,' she exclaimed and with a kick of her spurs, started the charge. A huge cry of 'Elora, Elora,' rang out as Roseanna and Isla immediately responded and the whole cavalcade of horses thundered across the ground. The earth shook beneath them. Roseanna, dressed only in black slacks and a black cotton top was standing up in her stirrups and leaning forward with her sword pointing straight at the enemy. She had a wild look in her eye.

'Avanti, Avanti!' she cried.

As she did so everything went into slow motion. She could hear the heartbeat of the horse beneath her and the relentless pounding of its hooves against the firm ground. The rhythmic sound sent her into a slow hypnotic trance where she was at one with the universe and everything in it. Still charging forward, she entered into a slow dance with time. Everything stood still and in her head she regressed back centuries to her charge at the battle of Caudine Forks in the Samnite wars against the Romans.

On that stirring day, the Samnites had seized a glorious victory against the mighty Roman army. For her bravery, Gavius Pontius, gave her lands on the rich slopes at the foot of the Apennine Mountains. Beautiful lands for her and her mother and father and family to farm. He had also honoured her for her great heroism during the battle by bestowing on her the title 'Rosa Volpe', Italian for the Red Fox, the name she was now known as in Maritania, Roseanna Fox.

On that day she had been fighting for her country against the invaders from the north. Fighting for her very existence. It was no different this day as she, like everyone else, was fighting for their future in body, spirit and soul in the real world they called home.

'Avanti, avanti!' she cried, as she rode like the wind, high in her stirrups with her sword aloft encouraging all to follow.

On the right-hand flank Isla was leading the charge just as strongly. She was inspired by Abi's rallying cry to open up a pathway to decency and justice. She had fought in many a battle for the Royalists against those who would like to have seized power. In those battles, whether the King's troops were defeated or victorious, it was the ordinary people on both sides who were always the ones that paid the ultimate price.

Today was different. Today she fought for herself

and those who stood beside her. The prize was their freedom to return to their own lives, in their own world. They had everything to gain and little to lose and that would give them the edge. She galloped on, keeping one eye on the flag and one on Abi to follow any commands she might signal.

When they were about four hundred yards from the enemy line, Abi noticed the scrones' army beginning to turn and go back over the drawbridge into the castle. As they did so, they started to get into a terrible muddle and all got in each other's way as they tried more and more desperately to get back over the drawbridge before the enemy was upon them. A large number of them realised they were not going to make it back into the castle in time and bolted off to the left heading towards the distant sea.

Roseanna made it clear to Abi that she would like to break off and chase after them. Abi, aware of what was happening, crossed her sword into her left hand and encouraged Roseanna to pursue them with all speed.

As the rest of the scrones finally made it over the drawbridge, it was wound up just in time behind them. Abi was aware that they had not retreated into the castle from fear, but under orders. Some plan was afoot. As Abi and her army came to a halt in front of the moat there was a sudden sound like a great rush of air. She looked up to see a cloud of arrows flying from the castle battlements that fell way over their heads onto the empty ground behind.

She was thankful that her assessment of the skill of the scrones in battle, based on the two she had met in the Summoner's visiting room, was proving to be accurate. Her army was still stuck however, with the drawbridge up, leaving them exposed out in the open where surely the scrones' archers would eventually find their range. Abi signalled to Isla to call the retreat and they all moved back a safe distance to assess what to do next.

***

Meanwhile, Will and Zach, along with Millie, had reached the headland and were making their way up the nearest, rocky side. It was very steep and both Will and Zach had to suck in deep breaths so that the blood would pump hard and fast around their bodies and keep their legs going up and up. In places it was so dense with trees they had to cut their way through with their axes. There were some treacherous pitfalls around the slippery sides of deep, water-filled chasms that they had to avoid, but eventually they emerged into the fresh air and the light, to climb the last fifty metres or so to the top.

Once they had rested for a short time, they selected some trees with branches which looked as if they would be ideal for the job of levering the rocks over the cliff face. They were just getting started with their axes when they heard a loud roar and pounding of the earth towards the very top of the headland. They both stopped and turned towards where the sound was coming from. It seemed that hey too had been betrayed.

Lumbering towards them, was a giant, monstrous beast about twelve feet tall, with huge, powerful flailing arms, breathing fire and gnashing its teeth. It was on a slow but sure path heading straight for them, roaring and wailing as its feet pounded the ground. The earth shook with every step as it came on and on down the headland towards them. Will could not imagine which creature Aquavena had transformed into this monster. Nowhere to run, he raised his axe and ushered Zach in behind him.

'Hold, in the name of humanity hold,' he cried. 'We are servants of the defenders of the righteous, carriers of light, bringers of peace. I besiege you hold.'

It was almost upon them and about to swipe its mighty arm and sweep them over the cliff, down onto the rocks and sea below when Millie flew at its feet and bit as hard as she could. While it was distracted, suddenly the big black wolf raced out from the trees and sunk its teeth deep into the monster's neck. Zach immediately recognised the wolf as the same one he had seen the other day when he was looking after the horses. The bright green eyes and the darkness of its coat were unmistakable. He fancied that it seemed to know him also, as for a brief second, their eyes met.

The beast roared in agony and kicked and flailed its arms about sending Millie flying backwards through the air. At the same time it was ripping at the wolf with its giant claws. They struggled and tore at each other so much that they didn't notice just where they were heading. In the next instant the monster went backwards over the cliff, taking the wolf with it. They floated down and down until there was an almighty crash as they both came to their end and lay dead on the rocks below.

Millie seemed to be relatively unscathed with only a slight injury to one paw which caused her to walk a little gingerly. Will and Zach felt sorry for the wolf, but they had no time to waste and soon set about hacking off the branches they had chosen for starting the rockslide.

***

Everything had gone quiet in the castle. There was no sign of movement anywhere and Abi began to wonder if the scrones, now depleted, had already made a break for it down the tunnel and out through the cave.

Isla approached and spoke briefly with Abi. Then Isla dismounted and started to walk towards the castle on her own. She moved slowly forward. All was quiet until she reached the halfway point when suddenly the next flight of arrows rained down. Isla quickly sank to her knees, tucked her head down and lifted her shield up in front and slightly above her. Three arrows thudded into it and for half a minute or so there was no movement to be seen from her. Then, just as Abi was beginning to think the worst, Isla sprang to her feet and ran back to safety as fast as she could.

There now seemed to be a stalemate as the scrones had a tight defence of the castle and Abi had no obvious way forward. Just as she was wondering what to do next, she looked up to the headland where Will and Zach had recovered from the monster's attack and were readying themselves to start the rockslide to block the entrance to the cave. She could just about make them out against the skyline. It looked as if Zach was waving frantically in the air at a looming massive, dark cloud that was appearing over the horizon. The more he waved, the larger the cloud grew and the closer it got to them. Zach was now dancing on the rocky outcrop, shouting in a rather wild, exaggerated voice:

'Fly you Canaries, fly up on high

Fly in your thousands and fill up the sky

Fly twenty leagues and seven leagues more

Fly o'er the ocean and fly o'er the shore

Weave your bright patterns in green and in gold

Weave your pure magic like 'strangers' of old

Fly you Canaries come gather ye round

Fly Canaries fly'

The huge cloud got larger by the second as it seemed to float over the headland and descend down towards the castle. It swirled and changed shape and got thicker and darker as it came down until finally, it engulfed the battlements and everything above them.

Abi saw her chance and set off towards the castle as fast as she could. As they reached the moat the scrones were being kept busy trying to understand just what had hit them. The canaries flew in massive numbers all around them so that they could hardly see a foot in front of their faces.

Before Abi realised what was happening and could stop her, Izzie had passed the flag up to her, unbuckled her sword and dived headlong into the moat. As soon as she did so, three of the largest alligators started heading straight for her. No matter how good a swimmer she was, it seemed certain they would catch her. Just as they were about to, the mass of canaries swooped down even lower, skimming the waters of the moat. The alligators reared up blindly into the air, snapping their great jaws in the hope of catching one. That gave Izzie just enough time to reach the other side. She hauled herself out of the water and ran to unhitch the lever that lowered the drawbridge.

As soon as it was down, Abi and Isla and all of their cavalry thundered across. The scrones, seeing they were now outnumbered, and having no real loyalty to their cause, turned and ran. As soon as Isla was over the moat she brought her horse to an abrupt halt, leapt off, and ran to make sure that Izzie was unhurt and to return her sword to her.

'Are you alright little one? Your bravery knows no bounds. Please permit me,' she said as she took the silver, gemstone brooch from her tartan plaid and pinned it on Izzie's tunic.

'Please accept this badge of honour on behalf of all who have fought here today. It was presented to me by the Marquis of Montrose after the battle of Auldearn and by tradition I now pass it on to salute the bravest of the brave.'

'Thank you Isla,' said Izzie, who felt truly honoured by Isla's concern. I will always cherish it. Your kindness and dashing, cavalier spirit will forever be my inspiration.'

The scrones had headed down into the bowels of the castle, along the service tunnel and out of the cave entrance. They were in such a rush they didn't even notice that the boat, which was for ferrying them in human form and for carrying supplies, was no longer there. They instead headed back to the Leviathan by immediately casting off their castle disguises and reverting straight away to the sea creatures that they were.

Being in fear of their lives, they had also failed to notice as they dived back into the sea, that the Leviathan wasn't in its usual place. It now sat some way beyond the headland under the joint command of Captains Jago Jelbart and Nico Dobben.

With the battle expected at the castle, the Leviathan had been left with only a skeleton crew of just a few scrones. The scrones were about as competent as sailors as they were as soldiers. Nico and Jago, with their crew of a dozen men had rowed out behind the Leviathan and boarded it on its least protected side. Jago then quickly scaled the rigging and stood high up on the yardarm. From his vantage point he grinned wildly and shouted out 'avast me hearties' and 'splice the mainsail' and other nautical terms he had never had occasion to ever shout before.

The sight of Jago sent shivers through the scrones crew. As they stood there transfixed, Nico and the rest of the small but gallant band, ran headlong at them armed only with broom handles. The scrones took one look at the charging mob and went straight overboard. Nico had already considered that jumping overboard, back into their own environment, would be much the preferred option for scrones. Not wishing to seriously harm them, he had opted for broom handles rather than swords. His assessment that broom handles would be enough of a threat, proved to be a wise one.

Having taken over the Leviathan, they had weighed anchor and sailed her to her new position just beyond the headland. They felt they would be slightly more hidden from the beach there, and that it would be easier to defend from all sides, should the need arise.

~ CHAPTER SEVENTEEN ~

The Battle: Part Two

More and more scrones raced out of the cave entrance and plunged into the sea to escape. When the last few had staggered out, Will and Zach began putting all their strength into levering some of the looser rocks immediately above the entrance. They crashed and tumbled down the cliff face carrying more rocks with them until, under their own momentum, they grew into a landslide. It was large enough to almost seal off the whole of the cave entrance. Only a small space near the roof was left unblocked. Will and Zach could hear the cheers of the crew on the Leviathan ringing out across the waters.

Back at the castle, a few had taken heavy blows and emerged bleeding from their combat as the scrones did their best to escape. They were being helped back out to where Loretta and Lucille were treating the wounded and assisting those who could no longer ride, onto the horse-drawn carts. The bandages were running low and Loretta, being the more forward of the two, gave Lucille a look that suggested there was nothing for it but to take desperate measures. She lifted her skirts and began to rip her petticoat into usable lengths. Lucille immediately followed suit and they were again able to applying dressings to the wounded.

Abi, Izzie and Isla were searching their way through each floor of the castle. They were looking to see if there was anyone in the dungeons or any scrones left behind, that they could round up. They reached the Summoner's office but there was no sign of him. Just as they were about to leave, Izzie noticed a door in the paneling of one of the walls. She pointed it out to Isla who got her sword at the ready and gingerly opened it. Inside was a little ante room and hanging up in the corner, near another door, was a red robe and a long piece of red cloth with gold trim. They all gave each other a knowing look, realising exactly what that meant. Moving swiftly over to take a closer look, Isla swung open the other door. They could clearly hear footsteps hurriedly making their way up the stone staircase.

Isla was off in a flash, closely followed by Abi and Izzie. The spiral staircase went up and up and up. As they climbed the final flight of stairs, they could see light flooding in from the open doorway at the top. When they came out onto the roof, swords at the ready, they saw that they were at the very top turret of the castle. Professor Fitzjohn stood high up on the battlement wall with one hand on the flagpole. He was dressed in a plain grey robe and stood smiling down at them as if he was pleased to see them.

'I would ask that you don't come any nearer,' he said. 'I have no wish to harm you in any way.'

'But why?' said Abi. 'Why have you been betraying us all this time?'

'You, of all people should know how it is Elora. The people are deliberately divided and exploited so that the few can control the many. They are taught what to believe to keep them in line so that they don't revolt. They are fed lies and all kinds of falsehoods to muddle their minds into believing that whatever they are told is the true way. Once they are signed up to that, they find it too difficult to back down and admit their folly. Even I, who understand this, am now entangled so deeply I have to continue or I will become the enemy and be hunted down. It is a circle that once entered into you will find impossible to get out of.'

As Abi was keeping him busy asking questions, Isla was slowly edging around towards him. He suddenly noticed her move a little closer.

'Don't come any nearer,' he warned her. 'I'll jump! Stay away I mean it, I'll jump.'

'Professor Fitzjohn,' said Abi in a sympathetic tone. 'We have no wish to harm you. I understand that you are a servant of Aquavena and had to do her bidding and no doubt the bidding of the Summoner also, but we offer you a way out. If you come with us we will help you to return to your rightful place among your own kind, whatever that may be.'

'No, no that can never be. If I were to betray Aquavena and the Summoner, I would never return to a normal life for fear of what they might do to me. Anyway, the time for all of you is not long. Very soon, in the final battle you will all be crushed.' His face then took on an even more sinister smile.

'Thank you my child but it is better that I settle this now, on my own terms, once and for all.' With that he let go of the flagpole, stood up straight and, still smiling, slowly leaned backwards and plummeted earthwards.

'Thank you Elora, we are one,' he cried in a mocking tone and then burst into loud, raucous laughter.

They had all rushed forward in an effort to stop him but he was already gone. They watched him falling down and down with the same serene smile on his face and his laughter echoing back up towards them.

Then, halfway to the ground, he suddenly spread his arms outwards and transformed himself into a giant eagle with huge, beating wings. He turned and soared upwards. As he passed them on the very top of the battlements, he thrust his mighty talons out towards them. At the same time he let out a great, eerie screech that pierced the air, right down into their very souls. He then gracefully turned away and flew off towards the headland and the sea, no doubt heading for the Mountain of Dreams.

~ CHAPTER EIGHTEEN ~

The Battle: Part Three

The three made their way back down and out onto the castle grounds where the rest of the troops were gathered. Every room had been fully searched, including the lower passageways and the dungeons, but it would appear that all the scrones had escaped as quickly as they could, back to their own natural environment.

Even the alligators in the moat seemed to have gone, most likely through an underground water channel straight out to sea. It crossed Abi's mind that as alligators can't survive in sea water, they too must have been scrones made for the purpose by Aquavena. By now they would have reverted back to whatever creatures they actually were.

They all crossed over the drawbridge and gathered

out on the grounds in front of the moat. The great canary flock had gone and the sun again filled a bright, blue sky with wisps of pure white clouds floating gracefully across it. Abi made sure everyone was lined up in proper order and then, when Izzie had the flag up and ready, she started a slow advance towards the sea.

It wasn't long before they were nearing the spinneys of trees. Abi was wary and took it slow and steady as they approached. She was relieved to find that if a trap had been set, it had now been abandoned. They worked their way through the trees and gathered once more on the other side. They then set off again in perfect order in another slow advance. On turning the last large bend in the open, grassy plain, they saw the sight they had hoped and prayed for. There, in the distance Abi, Izzie and Isla could clearly see Roseanna's battalion, just short of the seashore, with no opposition in sight.

As Abi and the flag came into view, a great roar went up from the shoreline. This was followed by rousing cheers of 'Elora, Elora' as Abi and Isla moved their troops into position alongside Roseanna. Roseanna then rode slowly down the line to Abi and bowed her head a little.

'Elora. We chased the scrones into the sea and they headed for the Leviathan but, as they approached they saw Nico, Jago and the others on board and swam around them and went further out to sea.' She bowed again and as she was returning to her position, the wind suddenly dropped and the sea became flat calm and eerily silent.

The whole line stood facing the sea about fifty yards from the water's edge. There was an odd whinny and the jingle of a bridle from one or two of the horses as they impatiently lowered and shook their heads. Apart from that, all sat silently awaiting the Elora's orders.

Just as she was about to declare victory and rally her troops, a little way out in the ocean she spotted two great horns moving towards her as they slowly rose up out of the still waters. She watched as the horns gave way to a silver war helmet and then below that, the huge smiling face of a bearded warrior began to emerge from beneath the waves. As it did so, just a yard in front of him, two silver ears broke the surface, closely followed by the enormous head of what looked like a giant, armoured, white horse. As it moved forward a few steps into shallower waters, it was apparent that this was no ordinary horse. It was at least twice the size of a normal, fully-grown horse and was clearly able to survive underneath the sea.

Abi instantly recognized it as a Kelpie. She had heard of these fantastical creatures before. They were said to live underwater in rivers and lakes and steal and eat babies. Up until now, she had thought of the Kelpie as just another mythical beast. There it stood, large as life, right in front of her.

As it moved a little closer into shallower water she could see that it was about half as big again as a normal horse. It was fully protected in silver armour and carrying the most enormous mountain of a man Abi had ever seen.

As the waters drained from him, he raised his right arm in the air. Slowly, all in unison, another one hundred or so mounted Kelpies rose out of the sea behind him. Each carried a similar giant of a man fully armed with a sword, shield and spear, all grinning from ear to ear.

For a moment or two, both armies just stood in silence looking at each other. Then, the leader of the Kelpie army began a slow, quiet chuckle to himself. He looked down and then up again at what faced him and his laughter became a little louder. He then turned to look back at his men and they all joined him until the whole air was filled with raucous laughter.

Suddenly, he raised his arm again and the laughter immediately stopped. Once more he looked down at the sea lapping around him and then he slowly lifted his head to look directly at Abi.

'I am Herodius, Poseidon's champion. Make peace with your God and prepare to die.' As he said this his army all lowered their visors, pointed their spears forward into the attack position and adjusted their shields to the defensive pose. Just as Herodius was about to signal the advance, Abi, out of the corner of her eye, caught a movement in her ranks out to her right-hand flank. She raised her hand and everything stopped as Isla slowly walked her horse up to her. Abi and Isla exchanged a few words. Then Abi looked Herodius up and down.

'You say you are Poseidon's champion. Rather than

bringing death and destruction on all here gathered, I challenge you to single combat, champion against champion.'

'Why should I spare your people, when I can annihilate all of you, whenever I want?' Herodius replied, still grinning widely. Abi stood her ground.

'Oh what a great warrior you are. Sounds like you are frightened of my champion and need your men to back you up.' Herodius' mighty laugh rang out again.

'Yes go on laugh,' said Abi. 'It is the action of a coward who hides behind his boasting but gets others to do his bidding. I challenge you. My champion awaits. Winner takes all.' With that Herodius dismounted, which only made him look even more enormous, and with his shield and sword at the ready took a few steps towards her.

'Well,' said Abi. 'Are we agreed?'

'Agreed,' he said as he turned his gaze towards Isla. 'Come, little one, prepare yourself for your final moments.' As he said this Isla dismounted. She then drew her sword and readied it in her right hand while holding her shield up in her left. She took a few steps forward and, now that they were a little closer to each other, she looked even smaller and more puny. Herodius, with a massive grin on his face, shook his head in dismay at the reckless folly of his opponent.

He stood his ground as Isla again started to walk towards him. When she got to around thirty yards from him, she suddenly threw her sword out onto the sands.

Herodius looked from the sword to the slight figure of Isla and then back again to the sword in confusion. As he did so, Isla raised her shield up in front of her and moved forward a little more. Herodius was even more confused as she advanced towards him. Leaving his shield down by his side, he raised his mighty sword above his head ready to split Isla in two. It was then Isla pulled her shield to one side and Herodius felt a great stabbing pain in the middle of his forehead, right between his eyes.

Isla was loading a second whirling stone but there was no need. Herodius stood stock still for a second or two. Then, his eyes closed and he fell straight down, face first, landing on the sand with an almighty crash at Isla's feet. It shook the whole beach so much that some of the horses reared up and became skittish with the strange vibrations that ran through the ground and up into their bodies.

There was a deafening, joyous roar from all along the shoreline. Instantly, the Kelpies of his army, having seen their champion defeated, transformed back into turtles and his soldiers into porpoises. They turned and all headed, further out to sea and away, as fast as they could.

As those on the shore watched them flee they could see some activity aboard the Leviathan. The anchor had been weighed and extra sails were being hoisted as it started to move further out into deeper waters. It was an impressive sight in full sail but it soon became clear that it was heading straight for one of the large whirlpools that guarded the entrance to the bay.

They all stared anxiously as it got closer and closer to the swirling waters. There was wild activity on the deck as the men ran to the stern of the ship and then seemed to disappear over the far side. As the Leviathan buffeted its way forward and was dragged into the maelstrom, the small rowing boat appeared, edging its way back in the direction it had come from.

The whirlpool became a boiling tumult of water and the Leviathan started to rock and roll and pitch and tear itself apart. Three majestic eagles came swooping in from the far clifftop and flew round and round the ship, screeching wildly in great distress. The masts one by one came tumbling down with loud crashing sounds of splintering wood, until the galleon was finally sucked under and disappeared into the depths.

As soon as it did, and it was clear that the rowing boat and its crew were safe from the whirlpool, a huge cry of 'Elora, Elora' once again filled the air. The crew raised there oars in salute as they headed back to shore.

Abi, sitting upright and proud on her beautiful stallion, rode out in front of her victorious army and raised her sword in the air.

'All hail our champion Isla.' There was a huge roar and waving and cheering from all around. Abi then raised her sword again and all fell silent.

'Citizens of Maritania. All journeys start with a single step and today, together, we have taken that step.

It has been a great victory in our quest to return to our own place and time amongst our friends, families and the ones we love. The battle is not yet won. Difficult days may still lie ahead. I urge you to have patience. With faith and fortitude all will be well. As for today, today is ours, let's be thankful and celebrate.'

With that there was a great cheer and Abi turned and led them back to the camp with great cries of 'Elora, Elora' ringing all around.

~ CHAPTER NINETEEN ~

The Celebration

Back in the camp, all readied themselves for a night of revelry and rejoicing after their victory. Those not able to fight had, on the Elora's orders, prepared a grand feast, fit for conquering heroes.

The refectory was fully lit with torches both inside and out and a group of minstrels played light, joyous music in tribute to those who had fought so bravely and had won the day. When everyone was assembled and all was ready, the first of the major players from the battle to come into the hall were Will and Zach, with Millie limping a little by Zach's side. They received a rapturous welcome.

Next came Nico and Jago with their team of sailors who marched in with their oars aloft chanting 'Elora,

Elora' as the crowd joined in. After them came Roseanna and Izzie. Izzie proudly carried the flag and waved it from side to side as she marched in. Roseanna strode forward behind her, wielding her sword, battle ready, and shouting 'Avanti, Avanti our beloved Elora'.

Just behind them came the two twins, arm in arm, bowing and gently smiling to the left and right as if they were born for such occasions, which of course they were. The crowd cheered and cheered until finally, Abi, with the crown of the Elora gracing her head and with Isla on her arm, came through the doors to a huge rousing cheer and the now familiar chant of 'Elora, Elora' raising the roof.

As soon as Abi reached the front, she turned and all went silent. Some had bowed and others had gone down on their knees in thanks and adoration.

'Arise, arise,' said Abi. 'We bow from politeness and respect but we kneel to no-one. We are one.'

'We are one.' the crowd immediately replied.

'I thank you all for this great victory today,' Abi continued. 'Each and every one of you played your part and each shall receive your reward in the time of the return, whenever that may be. Until then fear not and do not be anxious for your salvation. What will be will be, but in the final end, the righteous and virtuous shall prevail and all will be well. Eat, drink and be merry for the day is ours.'

With that the music began again and they all sat at the trestle tables as the meal was served up. Abi went from table to table to thank each of them more intimately. The other members of the Council, took their lead from her and followed suit. Before long there were handshakes and merry laughter all round.

Once the meal was finished, the central tables were removed from the hall and each of them took their drink and moved to those tables and benches around the outside, leaving a large, clear space in the middle. The music then changed to the fast rhythm of the balalaika and five athletic, young, Cossack fishermen from the hinterlands of the Black Sea, who had helped Nico and Jago sink the Leviathan, whirled and kicked and clapped and shouted in a rousing epic dance of celebration.

After that a young Spanish couple took to the floor. The man was immaculately dressed in tight trousers and a magnificently embroidered waistcoat. He danced with great energy and flamboyance, marking out the rhythm with the heels of his boots. A tall, slim, elegant lady, in a tight dress with a trailing frill, who had a rose in her hair and another in her mouth, danced around him seductively, her eyes flashing in the torchlight.

And so the night went on. Isla set out a pair of crossed broadswords on the floor and, with her hands held up in the air, thumb to forefinger, she performed an exquisite sword dance. She showed the same dexterity and swiftness of movement she had in the battle, her feet neatly skipping around in between the swords, but never touching the blades.

The euphoria began to give way to nostalgia and a

feeling of a longing for home. None more so than with Nico, who finished the evening's entertainment with a slow lament for the land he loved and missed so much. They all understood the sentiment no matter where they came from or where they called home. He waited until all was quiet and then, perched on one of the tables with his feet on the bench in front of him, in a deep, soft and tender voice he sang:

When the wind blows from the east

The day gives way to fading light

From German border to the sea

The autumn sky casts shadows wide

My mystery land, my Netherland

My mystery land, my Netherland

When the wind blows from the north

We light the fire and stay at home

When the wind blows from the north

The fields are white with snow

To cool my land, my Netherland

To cool my land, my Netherland

When the wind blows from the west
The waves are rolling in with pride
The sea reclaims what once was hers
A little more with each spring tide
To cleanse my land, my Netherland
To cleanse my land, my Netherland

When the wind blows from the south
We drink wine and we drink beer
When the wind blows from the south
The sun will shine now summer's here
To warm my land, my Netherland
To warm my land, my Netherland

When the wind finally dies down
And what has been has been
When the wind finally dies down
I close my eyes and dream
Of my father's land, my Netherland
Of my father's land, my Netherland

The beautiful song, with its sentiment of a longing for home wherever that might be, touched all of their hearts. It brought the evening to a close and left Abi in a deep quandary about the love of one's own country. Surely we can love our homeland and recognise that all people have a homeland and love theirs in just the same way. So why have there been so many wars around the world? Abi couldn't see the sense in it and wondered where the truth of it all might lie?

It struck her that birds fly the skies, fish swim the seas and animals roam the land, living side by side with their own kind, with hardly ever even a minor squabble. Humans, on the other hand, had carried out wars against fellow humans throughout history. Will noticed Abi deep in thought.

'What troubles you Elora?' he said. 'Anything I can do?'

'Nothing more than troubles you and the whole world and that is the truth of it,' she replied, giving him a wry smile as reward for his kindness and concern.

'I was just wondering why it is Will, that we humans have battles with humans all the time while birds, fish and other animals seem happy to live relatively peacefully in harmony with their own kind?'

'Greed,' said Will. 'The birds, fish and other animals are free to roam wherever they wish and they only take from nature's bounty what they need to live and survive on day to day. Man, on the other hand, has those among them who are full of greed and mistrust. They set up false walls and borders and spread delusions among their fellow man that those outside those walls and borders wish to take everything from them. They then encourage those inside to attack first or they will be doomed. And so it goes on.'

Abi thought about how all the nationalities she had witnessed here in Maritania were all working together towards a common cause in a land without greed or envy. A land without borders.

After a moment or two's further thought she came to the same conclusion Isla had come to many years before. Those who cause the mayhem and destruction are those least likely to suffer and most likely to prosper from it. The people who pay the price are those who have everything to lose and nothing to gain.

'What do you say Will? Do you think there are more scrones amongst us, others like Professor Fitzjohn who would spy upon us and betray us?'

'Who can tell?' replied Will.

'What about the Summoner. Do you think he might cause us more trouble?'

'No Elora. I think the Summoner will be long gone. He is the biggest fool and coward of them all. Those at the very top often are. They are put there by others to take the blame should things go wrong and when they do they are soon disposed of, never to be seen or heard of again. The world is full of fools who are but puppets. I do not blame them, I only pity them with their false, meagre lives.'

'What of the others? This Guide and this Herald you all speak of? If we capture them, do you think they will be able to lead us back to the Cauldron and out of Maritania that way?'

'It is most unlikely Elora. Once each of us were taken through the Cauldron by the Guide and were spoken to by the Herald, none of us ever saw them again. What is more, I have roamed this country over and over and I have never been able to find the Cauldron. It would appear it is a one way trip.'

'Appear?' said Abi. 'I am sure you know in your heart Will, nothing here is quite how it appears. All I know is it would appear that I was not summoned. It would appear that I am the Elora and it would appear I am the only one who has ever seen Aquavena. The answer to this riddle must lie somewhere with Aquavena and I must find her.'

'But we have searched everywhere and found no trace of her,' said Will.

'Then we must look where you have not searched. Like the scientists of old, we must look beyond the visible into the darkness to find the answers we are looking for. Beyond where we can see, into where we cannot see. Only then will we find truth.'

Will looked a little puzzled but not wishing to disturb her any further, once again thanked her for their great victory, excused himself, bowed and bid her goodnight. As he was taking his leave, Abi called after him.

'Thank you Will and all my blessings to you and to the big, black wolf that saved your life. It did us all a great service.'

~ CHAPTER TWENTY ~

Izzie's Song

Abi awoke to the new day in urgent mood.

'Isla, Isla, have you seen Izzie?' she asked. 'Do you know where she is?'

'Oh yes, she has gone to help feed the horses and more than likely have a quiet talk with her piebald, Thruppence.'

'Thruppence?' Abi repeated somewhat bemused. 'Is that its name?'

'Well, that's what Izzie called it yesterday in their long conversations during breaks in the battle,' replied Isla.

'Conversations?' said Abi, still bemused.

'They were rather one-sided but from what I heard, it would appear that young Izzie has a vivid imagination,' Isla replied with a smile. 'At one point she was asking Thruppence, about when the horses go out to fly at night, how do they manage to always find their way back into the right field in the dark? She then mumbled something about a homing device like pigeons.'

'Sounds like Izzie,' said Abi with a knowing smile.

Izzie's mysteriousness was the reason Abi so urgently wanted to speak with her. During the night, some of the song Izzie was singing as she walked along towards the castle on their first day in Maritania, came back into her mind. She had tried and tried but, as it is when you wake up in the morning, all the words of the song had just floated off one by one and disappeared. All she could remember was that the song might be important and she had quickly written a note on a piece of paper by her bedside to remind her to ask Izzie about it.

She soon made her way to the horse paddock and spied Izzie feeding young Thruppence a carrot, whilst engaged in a deep discussion with her, about whether she, or any of her descendants, had ever been to the St. Winnold's day horse fair.

'Izzie, Izzie,' Abi shouted as she approached. 'Everything okay?'

'Oh, hi Abi. I left you sleeping. Hope you don't mind. I thought you might need the rest, what with you carrying that crown around all day and everything. Only joking.' Abi put an arm around her little sister and gently kissed her forehead.

'I'm so proud of you Izzie. Next time you are going to swim a moat full of alligators, don't ask me first. I might just have said no, and then where would we be?' Abi smiled again and gave her another little hug.

'Izzie, can you think back to when we were walking from the moorings to the castle on our first day here. Do you remember the song you sang as you walked along? I mean do you remember any of the words? I didn't realise it at the time but something is telling me it could be important now.'

'What song? What was it about?'

'It was about things you see out in the fen like swans and ducks and things. Izzie didn't have to think twice.

'When you go walking in the fen, all on a summer's day. Does that sound like it Abi?'

'Yes that was it Izzie. Can you remember the rest?' Izzie, without any great thought, recited the song off the top of her head as if she had known it all her life. When she got to the verse that said:

'When the light shines on the waters

Every now and then

Horizons sometimes slip away

And then drift back again'

'That's it Izzie, that's the bit that ran through my head last night but it was gone before I could write it down this morning.

'Why do you think it might be important Abi?'

'Well I'm beginning to wonder about the light out here on the fen and about looking beyond the light into the darkness. Let me think on it a while and see if it leads me anywhere. We will be having a Council meeting later and I might talk further on it then. Thanks Izzie. Oh and by the way, why Thruppence?'

'Well Abi, I've always wished that I had lived in the days when people used the word thruppence on a regular basis. I mean some words are quite nice but thruppence, well, goes without saying, doesn't it. Nothing could be finer than getting your tongue around a word like thruppence. Just imagine as a young child getting thruppence for your pocket money. The world would be a much better place.'

It served to remind Abi, not that she needed reminding, just how strange at times her little sister could be and why she loved her so much. With that, Abi said she was off to find Zach and, more importantly, see how Millie's paw was bearing up.

She needn't have worried. Zach was throwing a ball about outside the blacksmiths forge. Millie, clearly fully recovered, looked as bright and lively as ever.

'Everything alright Zach?' she said as she bent down to make a fuss of Millie. She then stared up at him and he had a pensive look on his face as if he was not sure about something.

'Anything troubling you?' said Abi.

'Well, not troubling, but when Will and I were

attacked by that monster yesterday, the big black, green-eyed wolf suddenly came from nowhere to help defend us. I am sure it was the same wolf I saw down by the stream when Will was up on the rocks calling for Polly.

'I see what you are thinking Zach, with the startling green eyes and jet black fur and all, but I think it is too late now. The wolf is dead and I think it would be best to leave well alone?' Abi said this in a questioning way leaving space for Zach to reply.

'It was probably just my imagination anyway,' he smiled down at her.

'It wouldn't do anyone any good. Best let it lie,' said Abi as she stood up and gave him a small sisterly hug.

'Council meeting straight after lunch, see you then.' she said as she turned to leave. Then, ever thoughtful, to help erase the subject of the wolf from his mind, she stretched out a hand, tussled his locks and with a big, beaming smile, pointed up at the sky.

'Fly Canaries fly Zach. Fly Canaries fly.'

~ CHAPTER TWENTYONE ~

The Light on the Fen

They sat in the Council chamber all staring at the one empty chair. The paddle and the Priscus Percepta were no longer there and in their place, in the centre of the table, on a red velvet cushion, sat the Elora's crown.

'That treacherous rat,' said Jago. 'If e' was 'ere now, I'd ring 'is neck, I would, proper job.' Abi raised her hand.

'Be calm, Jago. As we know, he was under another's direction and only following orders. Without proof of his personal responsibility for his deceitfulness we must be merciful.' With that Abi pointed at the crown to bring everyone's attention to it.

'This is the crown of the Elora. Look upon it, look directly upon it. We are one. We are all the Elora. All of us together. All gathered here and all in the camp. I may wear the crown but all of us carry it together and share the weight of our great quest together. We are one.'

'We are one,' they all repeated in unison. Abi then went round the table thanking each of them for their heroic deeds during the battle, finishing with her thanks to Loretta and Lucille for the great sacrifice of their petticoats that had saved many a weary, wounded soldier. The twins blushed a little as smiles and applause rang around the room. As it tailed off, Abi gave them both a final, sincere glance of respect and admiration.

'Now on to other matters. Aquavena, have any of you ever seen her? Will tells me he has roamed far and wide and never found her, nor come across the Cauldron or the Guide or the Herald ever again. Is this true for all of you?'

'None of us have ever seen her,' Isla responded. 'Nor any sign of her, and none of us has seen the Cauldron, the Guide or the Herald since the day we arrived.'

'I have been thinking about this,' Abi continued. 'Although the Guide and the Herald could be hiding, it would be difficult to hide the whole area of the Cauldron, would it not?' Abi looked round for a reaction and was greeted by nods of agreement from all.

'If Aquavena can hide the Cauldron, by some magic or trick of the light, then it might also explain how the castle can appear to get bigger as you get closer to it and why the Mountain of Dreams can seem to disappear as you go towards it but, as we now know, not disappear if you stay at a distance. All of this makes me wonder if Aquavena, being queen of all the oceans, seas, lakes and rivers can use the reflections of the light out here on the fen to trick the eye, so that we only see what she wants us to see.' Nico nodded agreement and added that he had seen many strange, unexplained sights and apparitions when the sun was high in the sky over the waters of the Low Countries.

'Well that's all very well,' said Will. But sorry, I don't see how that will help us find Aquavena.'

Before Abi had time to reply, Roseanna burst in with a wild, excited look in her eye.

'I see, I see Elora. The only place we have never been is The Mountain of Dreams because it disappears as we approach it. That would point to the mountain being the most likely place where she will be.' Will, still puzzled came straight back at her.

'Yes, but how will we find her if we can't see the mountain and it disappears every time we approach it?' Roseanna looked straight at Abi and smiled deeply.

'We go at night, don't we Elora. We go at night when there is no light for Aquavena to trick us?' Abi gave Roseanna the kind of smile she usually reserved for Zach and Izzie.

'At night Roseanna, yes we go at night.' There was a hubbub of animated murmurings.

'What do you think dear?' Loretta addressed Lucille. 'Will you manage up a mountain in the middle of the night?' Just as Lucille was about to reply with words that no doubt would have implied anything Loretta could do, she could do too, Abi interrupted with her usual thoughtful foresight and discretion.

'I am sorry Loretta but I would like you and Lucille to remain in the camp, if you don't mind. Now Professor Fitzjohn has gone we need someone from the Council to make decisions back here if the need arises. Would you both be kind enough to do that?'

'Oh yes Elora, we don't mind, do we dear?' Loretta replied on behalf of them both.

'Oh and could you take care of Millie for us while we're away? I don't think it will be a suitable journey for her up on the mountain in the dark.'

'Yes of course dear,' said Lucille with a beaming smile.

'Any questions?' said Abi, looking around the room at everyone.

'When shall we go Elora?' said Isla.

'If we are all ready, we shall set off as soon as the sun sets tonight. We are one.'

'We are one,' they all replied.

~ CHAPTER TWENTYTWO ~

The Kingfishers

They had ridden in silence nearly all the way apart from the occasional whisper of instruction from Izzie into Thruppence's ear, the main one being, not to fly tonight of all nights. The rough ground in the dark made it slow progress as the torchlit procession wound its way up the path. It took them up and up and up until they were about halfway to the top of the mountain. There they came across a high wall with an iron gateway that crossed the path. Strangely, the gateway was open and a permanent sign above it, as part of the ironwork, read simply:

WELCOME

They carried on through the gate and about one hundred yards or so further on they could see a cave entrance. Beside the entrance there was a man sat by a fire. As they got closer Abi could clearly see that it was the Equerry. He was sat on a stone bench, sipping what looked very like a piping hot cup of tea. As they came up to him and made a stop, he simply raised his cup towards them a little.

'Welcome Elora, welcome,' he said with a genuine expression of sincerity in his voice. 'We have been expecting you. You must all be tired after your long ride. Please will you join me?'

Abi dismounted and the others followed her lead. She walked towards the Equerry and, as he stood up to greet her, she noticed that he didn't have his dark glasses or his white stick and his eyes were wide open.

'Was that all a trick then Equerry, pretending to be blind?'

'Oh no my child, I can't see a thing in the daytime. Besides, I am the Equerry, I treat all as I would wish to be treated and have no time for tricks, lies or deceit. I leave that to my superiors.' The Equerry laughed a little and then continued, 'I almost said to my betters, but no, I was right the first time. You have met the Summoner so I am sure you will understand what I mean. Not all who have ended up in the service of rogues and fools deserve to do so. Life does not always work out as you planned or as you would wish it. Don't be swift to judgement about those who somehow find themselves in the grip of scoundrels and blaggards. Fate can be a strange bedfellow and not everything is as you would like it or indeed as it would seem.'

Abi bowed her head slightly and offered up her hand which he gladly took.

'Please forgive me Equerry. Much is happening in my young life and sometimes I forget myself.'

'No need to apologise,' said the Equerry. 'Come, please, you are all welcome. Come take some rest.'

They all made their way over to the fire and sat on the stone benches, all except Roseanna that is. She had been deceived and betrayed so many times before that she was not as trusting as she would like to be. She raised a hand to signify that she was fine where she was and stayed with the horses a little way back in the shadows. The Equerry poured each of them a cup of tea and Isla took one over to Roseanna before returning to the light of the fire.

'Can I ask you something that has been puzzling me Equerry? Why is the Summoner called the Summoner when it is clear that it is Aquavena who does the summoning not him.'

'Oh well my child you know how it is. Some people are filled with their own importance and like to get above themselves. He is actually 'The Summoner's Director' responsible for processing those the Aquavena has summoned but he shortens it to make himself sound a little grander than he is.'

'Thank you Equerry, it was just something I noticed

that I couldn't explain and as you will know, the unexplained can be very annoying. You say you were expecting me Equerry. Why would that be?' asked Abi.

'The day you first arrived at the castle and said that you were not summoned, I had my suspicions. Then, when news came that the Elora was amongst us, I was pretty certain it would be you.'

'Yes, but why were you expecting me here at the Mountain of Dreams?' queried Abi.

'All roads on Maritania eventually lead here. Within its walls lies all the wisdom of the ancients. It is the final resting place for understanding and truth, and the conduit through which all conflict and unrest must be resolved. All the trials have been set before you and you have come through each with persistence, fortitude, humility and righteousness. Your time has come.'

'What do you mean my time has come?'

'Destiny has brought you here my child. Aquavena has selected you and tested you for the great task ahead. Many would have fallen by now but you are still here. Everything is as it should be and will be and the time is now. Aquavena awaits. With that he indicated that they should all enter the cave and make their way across to the middle of the bridge.

Abi didn't hesitate. She thanked him kindly and strode forward followed closely by Zach, Izzie, Will and Isla, with Nico and Jago following on. Inside was a massive chamber which reached up hundreds of feet and was open to a starlit sky above. The sky only served to bring to them the realisation that although it was well after midnight and dark outside, inside all was light.

Here and there, great fountains of sparkling water cascaded down the inside walls, bouncing off rocks and ending up in the lake below. On coming through the entranceway, the path led on to a stone bridge which crossed the middle of the lake over to the far side. There, it carried on straight into a curtain of water running down from the walls above. The water appeared to obscure behind it a hidden chasm in the rock.

Here and there in the lake were a few large rocks protruding boldly above the surface of the water. On one or two of these outcrops, flourished trees in full leaf, bringing a sense of splendour and serenity to the whole scene. All were amazed at what they saw and took a full minute or two to take it all in. Then they made their way to the middle of the bridge as instructed. Once there, they stood silently, waiting amidst the tumult of the water crashing around them. All of a sudden, the rush of the waters eased down and stopped. All was deathly silent. They each stared down into the watery depths below the bridge, not sure what would happen next. What did, shook Abi to the core.

The three blue lights appeared just as they had on that day in Downham so long ago. They were in the same formation with one in front and two behind. They moved out thirty feet or so from the bridge and then the beautiful iridescent blue lights started to spin until they formed three perfect blue circles, about ten feet in diameter, just above the water.

They all stared at the circles wondering what they could be and as they did so the water within the circles started to vibrate violently. The rest of the water outside of the blue circles stayed perfectly still as that inside the rings became so turbulent it looked like it was boiling.

Slowly, from the depths, three figures began to rise up through the blue rings. They were instantly recognisable as Aquavena and her two servants. They appeared just as they did on the flag. When they stopped, the water below their feet went calm and they stood directly on the surface just as if it was solid. Even more strangely, they didn't appear to be wet. Next, the blue circles of light broke away and took off on their own, each heading in a different direction.

At last, after all the years that Abi had pictured them in her mind, she finally knew what the lights were. The kingfishers each flew to a different tree and perched on a branch as if they were awaiting further instructions.

"Of course, of course," thought Abi. *"They were Aquavena's guides. That's what they were. They were kingfishers and as I looked down from the bridge at them flying ahead of Aquavena and her servants, the sunlight was bouncing off their brilliant, iridescent blue feathers."*

This revelation so filled Abi's mind that she stood stock still whilst the others had all taken a step back in shock at what they were witnessing.

Aquavena looked exactly as she did on the flag

except that in real life her face took on a softer, less menacing demeanour. This was in stark contrast to her servants who looked more scary and frightening in the flesh. Aquavena held out an arm and they both slowly sunk back down out of sight into the deep waters below.

Abi was still entranced by the revelation of the kingfishers. She was so convinced in her mind that the lights must have been emitted from some mechanical device that to find out otherwise, left her deeply amazed. She was suddenly brought back to reality by words she was not expecting to hear. In a commanding and very deliberate voice Aquavena addressed her directly.

'So Abigail Storm, we meet again so soon.' Abi was taken aback.

'What do you mean, meet again so soon. What meeting do you mean?' she demanded in a very inquisitive manner.

'Why in the channel, by the bridge in Downham. I waved to you and you waved back.'

'But that was years ago, when I was just a small child,' said Abi.

'As you have witnessed Abigail Storm, time is not in your hands. In the long history of time, what to you might seem an age, may to others only be a split second. In Maritania you have shared space and time with others from the distant past and perhaps some from the stretch of years that lie ahead. Time and space are not absolute. What has been and what is still to come are unknown to you and just like the Mountain of Dreams and the Castle and the Cauldron, time and space are dimensions beyond your control.'

'That may be true,' said Abi as she turned towards Zach and Izzie. 'However, unlike the others we are not under your control. We were not summoned to Maritania by you.'

'Summoned or not, do not rush to judgement,' said Aquavena. 'Zach was sad and disconsolate when he saw my eagles carrying the fish. He assumed it was their last journey but in fact they were being brought here to their safe spawning grounds so that they would not be fished to extinction. It is the same out in the real world. Often what you see is quite the opposite of what is actually taking place. As young people, new to the world, you must seek out truth in all matters and fight injustice wherever you may find it. Be careful, trickery and deceit abound.'

'I heed your wise words Aquavena, but why have you brought those who have been summoned here to Maritania?'

'My oceans, seas, lakes and rivers have been threatened. Some stole my seas from me and cut me off from them. Some polluted my waters with oil and waste and poisoned my streams with sewage and chemicals. Some fished and hunted my creatures into extinction, destroying their habitats so that they could never return.

'I have brought them here to stop some of the destruction and also as a punishment to those who have carried it out. The world has three living systems, the land, the water and the air. They all need care and protection from those who would exploit them. As queen of the waters it is my duty to do all I can to maintain the waters as best I can for the benefit of all.'

'And is this summoning of people to Maritania working?' said Abi in a questioning voice. 'Are your waters any better than they were? I think you are simply punishing the servants for the misdemeanours of their masters. Those responsible will simply get others to do their bidding and go unpunished. That will not stop the harm to the oceans, seas, lakes and rivers.'

'And what do you suggest Abigail Storm?'

'All in Maritania must understand the importance of why they were brought here. The part they played in the destruction of your waters and why they have been punished for it must be made plain to them. However, those who carried out the destruction are rarely the cause of it.

'I think if the people you have summoned here are made to understand that if they don't hold to account the selfishness and greed of the people responsible for the pollution and destruction of the land, the sea and the air, then they, and more importantly their children, will have no future. Keeping those who have learned that lesson held captive here will do nothing to protect your waters.

'If you send the people of Maritania back to their lands and seas to spread the word about what they have learned and to expose the people who would sell their children's future for profit, then, and only then will you have any chance of a better world for you and all of your creatures to live in.

'We could each swear an oath that if you return us to our home, we would do all we can to work towards a better future for you and all your creatures. If any of us ever break that promise, then you could recall them to Maritania at any time. Surely it would be better for you if we were all back out in the world doing all that we can to work on your behalf rather than being stuck here doing nothing?'

'You speak wisely for one so young Abigail Storm. I can see your straightforward words playing out well in the world. Sometimes the plain and simple truth spoken with the innocence of the young carries more weight than the most eloquently put doctrines of their elders. I can see that if the world had more young people like you spreading the word about their children's future and the future of the land, the seas and the air, it would be a good thing.'

Aquavena paused. In the silence that followed, there was a great weight of expectation.

'I will agree to your request, but I warn you all, have a care. The breaking of the promise by any one citizen of Maritania will mean a return here for all.'

Abi turned to Jago, Nico, Will and Isla. They all smiled and nodded.

'We accept,' said Abi. 'On behalf of all those summoned to Maritania, our grateful thanks. It is a long journey back so we shall return later this evening to take the oath and make the journey home.'

'No Elora. Your people will need more time to prepare and it would be easier in daylight. I am sure you will not mind spending one more night in Maritania. You can come during the day tomorrow. The Mountain of Dreams will be here for you, I promise.'

'That would be most helpful Aquavena. I thank you again.'

'Until then,' said Aquavena and with those words, she sank back down into the waters and slowly disappeared. Abi turned and they all embraced her and embraced each other. Isla then hurried out. She headed straight for Roseanna. Roseanna threw her arms around her and buried her head in Isla's shoulder, weeping deep, convulsive tears of joy. The thought of being back home with family and friends on the sunny slopes of Italy overwhelmed her.

Abi and the others came out to be greeted once again by the Equerry, who had noted the reaction of Isla and Roseanna.

'Success, if I'm not mistaken Elora? When will you be off?'

'Tomorrow Equerry,' Abi replied. 'We will see you again for the last time tomorrow afternoon. I am grateful for all you have done for us.'

'Well you may see me then, but I will not see you,' said the Equerry with a knowing smile.

'Why Equerry? Will you not be here tomorrow?'

'Oh I will be here, but as I said, I can't see a thing

in the daytime.'

'Oh I beg your pardon,' said Abi. 'I had forgotten about that.'

'No matter my child. Ah well never mind, back to the old routine under the river bank from tomorrow. I quite enjoyed my time as Equerry. A position in the world, a uniform, a little formality, a small modicum of respect. But I have to admit, all that is not what it is cracked up to be. Too much bowing and scraping and having to listen to idiots who think they know more than you do. Worse still, having to pretend that they know more than you do, so that you can trick them into thinking, that what you wanted was what they wanted, and that they thought of it first. It's all very tiring my dear, as you no doubt will find out, but all in good time. You must enjoy your younger years before that old merry-go-round begins. You will know what I mean when you get there. Now I think on it, a little eel time relaxing in the shadows under the far bank is probably just what I need.'

'I'll say my farewells again tomorrow Equerry, goodnight,' said Abi. With that they all raised a hand, mounted up and headed off back down the track.

~ CHAPTER TWENTYTHREE ~

Farewell Thruppence

They arrived back at camp just after breakfast. Within minutes of their return they rang the bell that brought everyone hurrying to the main building to hear the news.

As soon as the crowd had gathered, Will asked for silence and briefly explained all that had happened at the Mountain of Dreams. He then told them that, as long as they were willing to take the oath to do all they could to protect the oceans, seas, lakes and rivers for the sake of their children and their children's children, then they could return home.

The camp immediately erupted with excitement. People ran and hugged each other. Cheers and celebrations could be seen and heard everywhere. The women cried and so did the men, and chants of 'Elora,

Elora' could be heard all around.

The Bhats, on hearing the commotion, came out to get the news and to return Millie to Zach. As Zach was telling them all that had happened, Loretta and Lucille just stood there making the odd, 'Yes dear' and 'Oh I see' comment now and again. It was as if they didn't realise quite what he was saying. When he had finished they thanked him for letting them know and he thanked them for looking after Millie. They then turned, walked back up their small garden, went into their house and closed the door. There they turned towards each other.

'I think we should do our hair dear,' said Loretta.

'Yes dear, I think we should,' said Lucille.

They stared at each other for a few seconds. Their hands met as the tears welled up in their eyes. The hope that had been locked up and kept in check for so long, poured out and they hugged and cried together like they hadn't done since they were about nine years old.

Outside, the crowds were getting bigger by the minute. Nico and Jago walked down to the main building and rang the bell again. Then Nico nailed a sign to one of the posts by the main door. It simply read:

Assemble here at first sunrise tomorrow.

Bring everything you need for the journey home.

Elora – 'We are one.'

Abi, Zach, Izzie, Roseanna, Nico, Isla and Will, along with others in the camp, had just one more painful duty to perform. Some had established long and trusting, partnerships with their horses and now those had to be brought to an end.

Abi and Izzie, due to the immediate intensity of the battle, had built up very close relationships with their mounts in a very short time. That being so, they would suffer the pain of departure just as much as the others.

They gathered at the paddock and each checked their horse over and put on a bridle to walk them out as far as the grassy plain. Those horses without a particular handler, followed on.

Will led the way with Roseanna and Isla behind, watery-eyed. In an effort to lighten the mood Will quipped as he went.

'Your lucky day my chestnut beauty. Never will you have to hear my singing again.'

Will's words caused Roseanna and Isla to raise a smile but try as he might, they could not overcome the sadness they felt at saying goodbye to their brave mounts who had fearlessly carried them into battle. Behind them came Abi.

'There my beauty, my grateful thanks to you for your noble service,' she whispered as she walked along patting her stallion on the shoulder. 'Soon you will be free. Free to choose your own path. Free to roam without borders. Today is your day for rejoicing as ours will be tomorrow.'

FAREWELL THRUPPENCE

Behind her, Izzie was giving Thruppence a good, strong lecture.

'Now listen Thruppence. I hope you will always behave properly now that you can do what you like. I mean, I know you're only small, but I don't want to hear about you bullying those that are even smaller or getting up to any mischief. Don't be a donkey. Do you hear me?

'And Thruppence, when you are out flying at night, that's if you do go out flying at night, and to be honest I'm not entirely convinced that you do, have a care and watch out for molehills on landing, they can be a bit of a hazard. Moles have little consideration for those trying to land on their rooftops in the dark.

'And Thruppence, don't go fraternising with those foxes. They will only outsmart you and if you go trying to outfox a fox, well you know how that's going to end up. The clue is in the name. They are just much too clever for you. Sorry, but they are. I'd steer clear if I were you. What's that Thruppence? Me? What am I going to do?

'Well, since you ask, I think I might decide to become famous at some point. I mean, as far as I know Downham Market hasn't produced any Olympic gold medalists, Nobel prizewinners or Booker prizewinners so I guess the odds must be shortening in my favour.

'My mother is a swimming coach at the Downham Leisure Centre just down the road. She taught me to swim long before I could walk or so she tells me. I can see myself doing a tumble turn on the last length of the

Olympic 800 metres freestyle final and meeting the Australian and USA swimmers as they are still coming up the other way.

'Either that or I might go down the science route and invent a new process that will completely reverse global warming overnight and pretty much single-handedly save the planet. On the other hand, I might decide to win the Booker prize and write a stunning bestseller that will take the world by storm, Isabella Storm, and be turned into a musical with a record-breaking run in the West End. I really don't know Thruppence? There's just too much choice.

'Anyway, I'm sure you'll have a nice time out here, eating what you fancy and going wherever you feel like going. I mean let's be honest, who wouldn't. Oh and if I was you, I'd make friends with Abi's stallion there, the big shiny, black one up front. He looks like the kind of friend you just might want on your side now and again. Not that I think you will ever need to take sides now humans aren't involved, but you never know.

'Oh and by the way, thanks for letting me call you Thruppence. I know it's not really your name but it's helped me fulfil an ambition of mine to say the word thruppence just as often as I want to, at least for a little while.'

They soon reached the grassy plain, where they all gathered together and removed the horses' bridles. Abi then took the lead and gave her stallion a good whack on its hindquarters.

'Ya, ya!' she shouted at the top of her voice. The stallion ran and jumped and kicked its hind legs in the air and then charged off down the open plain. All the others, in one glorious stampede of joyous freedom, raced after him and then gambled about and finally settled down or wandered off to investigate wherever the mood took them.

When they returned to camp, it was a hive of activity. Food was being prepared for an early morning start and belongings were being sorted and packed ready for the long walk ahead of them.

All of those who had been to the Mountain of Dreams that day were exhausted. Despite how tired they were, in bed that night, each of them lay awake hoping and praying nothing would go wrong and they would all be home soon.

~ CHAPTER TWENTYFOUR ~

The Portal of Time

An hour before sunrise the bell outside rang.

'Wake up Abi, wake up,' said Izzie, giving Abi a gentle shake. 'It's time to get ready.'

'Ooooh thanks Izzie, thanks. I could have slept for a week,' said Abi as she stretched and yawned herself awake. They could hear the crowds outside gathering in anticipation of the sunrise. The citizens of Maritania had waited a long time for this day and the excitement was already rising.

'Well, today's the day Abi. How are you feeling?'

'I shall feel better when it is all over and everything has gone as Aquavena promised,' said Abi.

She was soon dressed and sat on the bed.

'Can you pass me my shoes please Izzie?'

As she did so, Abi leaned forward and crossed her legs to put on her socks. She looked up at Izzie from under her fringe.

'What about you Izzie?' she said.

'Well, of course I, like you, am hoping everything will soon be back to normal but I am going to miss everyone, especially Roseanna, Nico, Will and Isla. Yes I shall really, really miss Isla,' she said as her voice drifted away and then it suddenly lifted again. 'Oh and Thruppence of course, mustn't forget Thruppence, though I'm sure she is much better off without me.'

They went through and had a little to eat and drink with Isla who was already packed and ready to go.

'How long do you think it might take to get there Isla,' asked Izzie.

'Well it took about four hours on the horses at walking pace so, when you consider some of our more elderly brothers and sisters I guess anywhere between six and eight hours. As long as we leave on time I would hope to get there by early to mid-afternoon.'

When they were all ready, Isla strapped her shield to her back and bundled her broadswords, along with the few small, personal items that she could manage to carry, into her flag.

Abi and Izzie had very little they needed to take with them. Isla came through with their beautifully decorated swords and helped them put them on. She then took the cloaks Abi and Izzie had worn in the Sacred Ground and tied them around each of their shoulders. Next she came through with the crown of Elora on its red, velvet cushion.

'We can't have the Elora without her crown now, can we? Not on this day of all days,' she said. Izzie took the cushion from her and was about to kneel down to present it up to Abi, but before she could, Abi went down on one knee and laughed. Izzie immediately handed the cushion back to Isla, lifted the crown from it and full of giggles, leaned forward, kissed Abi on the cheek and placed the crown on her head.

'All rise Elora,' she said in a pompous, mocking tone. And as Abi did so, while trying her best not to laugh too much, Izzie continued in the same joyous and fun-filled tone.

'We are one.'

All three of them laughed and laughed and hugged and laughed and then did their best to keep a straight face and adopt a more serious air as they were about to open the door and go outside.

'Are you ready Elora?' asked Isla as she was about to try turning the door handle for a second time. All three of them burst out laughing again.

As they stepped outside a huge roar of 'Elora, Elora' erupted from the throng of citizens all ready and waiting to go. Millie, who had been sat beside Zach, sprang to her feet and rushed up to Abi and Izzie, leaping up, full of excitement. Zach went over and calmed Millie down a little and then put her on her lead.

'There, there Millie,' he said as he smoothed her ears down on either side of her face. 'Don't tire yourself out. We have the long journey home ahead of us. Good girl, good girl.'

Abi, along with Izzie, Zach, Isla and Roseanna made their way to join Will, Loretta and Lucille at the front of the procession. Nico and Jago waited where they were to join on at the end as it passed by. They were there to make sure that all went smoothly in front of them and that no-one was left behind.

As they moved off and left the camp, the sun had just come up over the horizon and its golden rays were beginning to creep their way across the land. Its journey illuminated silvery patches of water, along with rocky outcrops on the headlands and shimmering, rustling leaves on the windward side of the odd, isolated tree.

Abi had invited Loretta and Lucille to be at the very front because she felt they should have that place of honour due to their long and distinguished service on the Council. There was also the more practical reason that they, being of a certain age, were probably the most appropriate to set the right pace for everyone else. All would stop to rest when the twins stopped to rest and start again when they started again.

As they walked along, Will, Isla and Roseanna said very little. They had waited so long for this day that they were frightened that somehow, if they said the wrong thing, it might just disappear. It would all be a dream or a hoax, and the Mountain of Dreams wouldn't be there.

When they did speak, they spoke of trivialities such as the weather. In actual fact it happened to be a fine day with nothing of note. There was no gale or storm or any extreme of hot or cold. Thankfully however, like most people, they were well practised in discussing the weather endlessly, even when there was nothing to discuss.

Another subject used to take their mind off of what was to come was the wide variety of birds that inhabit the fen. There was some debate about how long the Great Crested Grebe, the Pochard and the Goldeneye could stay under the water for, but it was soon forgotten when eight or nine of the huge eagles appeared, circling overhead. Since the incident with Professor Fitzjohn, there was a wariness whenever eagles approached. Isla had her whirling stones at the ready but thankfully, having shown only a passing interest in the procession, the eagles soon headed off over the higher peaks out towards the sea. The procession was just about to leave the rocky area, when, as before, they turned the corner and the Mountain of Dreams came into view. Even those who had seen it many times before had never seen such a welcoming sight.

The line halted for a rest and most also took the time to have something to eat and drink, to keep them going on the last leg of their journey. Anxious to reach their destination, they didn't rest for long. After only half an hour or so, they came to the point where the mountain had previously disappeared for Abi. As she passed it by and the mountain stayed where it was, a cheer went up that rippled its way like a giant wave of sound all the way back down the line.

Shortly afterwards they came to where the path started to rise up and work its way around the side of the mountain. Although the path was rising steadily, there was no let up as Loretta and Lucille pushed on ever upwards and onwards. Occasionally little bursts of song would ring out from certain sections of the march to help keep everyone stepping out positively towards their goal.

Then, all of a sudden, as they came around a bend in the path, they could see the gate just a little ahead of them. They were very pleased to see that it was still open. As the front of the line came up the last one hundred yards or so, the Equerry was there, this time in his formal dress, wearing his dark glasses and holding his white stick. They came to a halt in front of him and Abi took him by the hand.

'Thank you for meeting us Equerry. I appreciate your kindness.'

'Not at all Elora. Just doing my job. How was your journey? And who do we have here with you?'

'Loretta and Lucille,' said Abi as she put the Equerry's hand in theirs.

'Oh it has been such a long time,' said the Equerry with a slight tremble in his voice. 'Two of the finest and most dignified and upright ladies ever to honour us with their presence. Lovely to meet with you again.'

'Likewise Equerry,' replied Loretta with the most gracious of smiles.

'Yes, yes, likewise,' repeated Lucille. 'You are a true gentleman and we shall always remember your great kindness and understanding.'

With that Will, Isla, Nico, Roseanna and Jago also paid their respects to the Equerry who, true to his word had treated them all, and everyone else who had been summoned, with good grace and respect.

'And how are you young miss?' he said when he was again re-united with Izzie. 'Still full of fire and brimstone I hope?'

'Oh yes indeed sir, but I hope you didn't find me too rude?'

'No, not at all. I believe a rebellious spirit in the young to be a very good thing. Too many just go along with the flow these days, never questioning the status quo and, most strangely of all, somehow believing that grown-ups know best, when all the evidence so far would suggest otherwise. Take a look around you at wars, famine and the destruction of the land, the sea and the air. It is the children and the children's children who will suffer if those who have the power to make changes don't heed the warnings and turn away from the mistakes of the past. Today's children are our only hope for the future. There is much to be rebellious about and I would encourage you to maintain your young spirit. No matter who might tell you otherwise.'

'Thank you Equerry. I will do my best to always act

on your wise words.' said Izzie. With that, the Equerry had a pleasant exchange with Zach and then invited them to take their place at the middle of the bridge inside the mountain.

Everyone followed on, many shaking hands and having a friendly reunion with the Equerry as they went. They spread out, ahead of and behind the Elora until they were all inside and the bridge was full. They were amazed at the sheer size of the lake and the mountain that rose up above it, and at the loud roar of great fountains of cascading water here and there, as it poured down the inner walls.

All at once the water stopped, the noise died down and an eerie silence filled with anticipation took hold. This time, a single kingfisher darted out and flying round and round at great speed, its iridescent blue feathers painted a circle just above the water. Inside the circle, the waters shook and bubbled as before and great gasps filled the chamber as the circle disappeared, the waters returned to a smooth perfectly still surface and Aquavena rose up from below and stood before them. The deathly silence returned as Aquavena and the Elora faced each other.

'Abigail Storm, I have tested you against deceit and trickery, against might and power, against myth and magic and never once did you yield to temptation and take the easy route. You have always shown great courage and acted with honour and mercy towards others. You have passed all the tests set before you. I hope and pray that you will go out into the world and do what you can to help put everything back into balance, on the path towards harmony and salvation.

'Citizens of Maritania! Are all here gathered willing to swear the oath that on your return you will do all you can to protect the oceans, seas, lakes and rivers from degradation and destruction and help return them to clean, unpolluted waters to safeguard all of my creatures from death and extinction?'

'Yes Aquavena,' said Abi. 'We are one.' The crowd all then repeated 'We are one.'

'If that be so, then you may return back to the exact time and place you were summoned and, when you do, you will not have any memory of Maritania and never think of it again. Only the pledge will stay with you, but I warn you all, if any one of you willingly break your pledge, then all of you will be brought back to Maritania forever.'

Again Abi exclaimed 'We are one,' and all repeated 'We are one.'

'To return you must pass through the Portal of Time at the far end of the bridge,' Aquavena continued. 'To confirm that you accept the oath, each of you must reach up and touch the centre stone on the Portal before stepping through into the chasm beyond. Let the return begin.'

The Equerry had made his way to the Portal and the Secretary, the young lady dressed in the twin piece suit wearing heavy lipstick stood beside him, ready to assist.

He invited those nearest the portal to go through and the exodus began.

There were many farewells, handshakes, hugs and parting tears but as they stepped through, these gave way to the faint sounds of the normality of everyday life and then silence.

After a good length of time, all had gone through except the members of the Council who had waited patiently as duty dictated. First of them to take his leave was Jago. There were no hugs or tears, they were not his style.

'Farewell,' he said with a small tip of his head, and popping his pipe back into the corner of his mouth, he reached up, touched the stone and stepped through.

Next Loretta and Lucille said their goodbyes. They kept their emotions in check in public as they had been taught to do since birth. There were handshakes all round, and a pat for Millie. They then both, despite themselves, kissed Abi on the forehead and said bless you my dear, before each touched the stone and stepped through. On the instant they did, Loretta's familiar voice could just be heard.

'Isn't it a beautiful day Lucille? The garden is looking so lovely. Shall I ring for tea?'

Next to leave was Roseanna. She put on a brave face and thanked each of them with a hug and a kiss on both cheeks. Then she reached out and held Abi's hands in hers.

'Goodbye, Elora. Whatever the Aquavena says, I

will never forget you. The flame that burns so brightly within you will always be in my heart. We are one.' With that she turned and stepped quickly and nimbly through, touching the stone as she went.

'Arrivederchi!' she cried, and was gone.

Isla and Nico then looked nervously at Abi.

'I am sorry Elora but Nico and I will not be able to return,' Isla said tentatively.

'What do you mean Isla?' said Abi in a shocked voice. 'You must leave.'

'We cannot Elora. We are prisoners of war, working out on the fen, draining Aquavena's lands. If we continue, as we will have to do or die, the oath will be broken and all the others will have to return.'

'We cannot do that,' said Nico.

Abi turned to the Equerry and the Secretary.

'My understanding is that Aquavena's words were "If any one of you willingly break your pledge." Surely, if you are forced to break your pledge on pain of death, then you do not do so willingly. Indeed it is against your will, is it not?' The Equerry instructed the Secretary to check the wording in her notebook.

The Secretary turned to the relevant page and quickly read it through.

'The Elora is correct in every detail Equerry. Those were Aquavena's exact, particular words.'

'In that case, all will be well. Aquavena says precisely what she means, no more and no less. You may leave without fear of consequences.'

With that Isla and Nico thanked the Equerry and then turned and hugged and said their goodbyes to each of the others in turn. Isla had special words for Izzie and made her promise she would take a journey to the land of the Alban to see its beautiful mystery for herself one day. Nico and Isla then hugged Will and said their goodbyes. Before Isla's tears could fall, they reached up and touched the stone and stepped through into the chasm together. Will then looked the Equerry up and down a little nervously as if something was puzzling and worrying him.

'Equerry, can I also ask if I heard Aquavena correctly when she said we would return to the exact time and place we were summoned?'

The Equerry again consulted with the Secretary. She looked it up and had no hesitation in telling him that was precisely what she had said would happen.

'Why do you ask?' he said.

'I must know that my Polly will be there for me on my return, just as she was before I was summoned, and not left behind here in Maritania. I have always believed she is here somewhere and I would rather that the stars fall from the sky and the sun never rise again above the horizon, than leave my Polly behind and be forever without her.'

Zach, not wishing to give away any inkling of his own thoughts on the matter, bent down and turned his attention to Millie.

'Fear not,' said the Equerry. 'If indeed Polly has

been here, everything that has happened on Maritania will be left behind and will be unknown to you and to her. The only thing that will be retained is your allegiance to the oath, even though you will have no memory of where that allegiance has come from. As long as you keep your promise, life will continue for you just as it would have done if you had not been summoned. Everything will be just as it was.'

'It will be so,' said Abi. 'That is what was agreed.'

'I have trusted you so far Elora and I have no reason to doubt your word now,' said Will. With that he bowed, taking Abi's hand and kissing it as he did so.

'Thank you for everything Elora,' he said as he took a step backwards. He then turned and smiled at Zach and Izzie for one last time.

'My true love awaits and I must fly,' he said as all in one action he reached up, touched the stone, shouted farewell and leapt through into the chasm.

That left only Abi, Zach, Izzie and Millie still to return.

'Before you depart,' said the Equerry to Abi. 'I would like to give you a message from Aquavena. She asked me to convey to you that her threat to return everyone to Maritania if anyone broke their oath was not to be taken seriously. She does not believe that the many should be punished for the failings of the few, but knows from past experience, that if people know that others will be punished for their misdemeanours, they are much less likely to make them. She apologises for this small deceit but feels that, in this instance the ends justify the means. She asks for your forgiveness?'

'Please tell her there is nothing to forgive.' said Abi.

Well, Elora,' said the Equerry in his usual sincere and kindly manner. I am sorry to have to put it this way but I hope we never see each other again.'

'Yes indeed Equerry. That would be more than unfortunate,' Abi replied with a telling smile. 'Before we go, I do want to thank you for your courtesy and for your wise words. They will remain with us and I am sure help to guide us as we make our way in the world. We will at all time do our best to follow Aquavena's lead and help protect the waters, and the land and air, for the sake of our children and our children's children.'

Abi then took off her crown and her cloak, unstrapped her sword and handed them to the Secretary who put them on a small table that stood behind her. Izzie and Zach could see that they also would have no use for their swords after their return and, following Abi's lead, undid their sword belts. As Izzie did so, she unhooked Millie's lead from her wrist and laid it on the ground. The instant she did, Millie turned and raced off as fast as she could back over the bridge.

'Millie! Millie!' they all shouted after her, each knowing in their hearts that they could not return without her. 'Millie! Millie come back!'

Millie kept on running and they all went chasing after her. She had ran over the bridge with her lead trailing along behind her. They were all running as fast as they could and shouting after her to stop. They were running and shouting and running and shouting and running …

#

~ CHAPTER TWENTYFIVE ~

No.8 The Old Bookshop

'Izzie, Izzie. Come on Izzie, else we'll be late home.' The words came from Abi as she took hold of Izzie's shoulder and gave it a little shake. It was just enough to bring her back into the here and now. She had been peering into No.8 The Old Bookshop window and she slowly turned to see Abi and Zach smiling warmly at her.

'Did you see them Abi?' asked Izzie.

'See who?' said Abi.

'The lady in the black cloak with the crown on her head and the very tall man with dark glasses and a white stick.'

'Who? Where Izzie?' said Abi in a bewildered tone

'There, moving around and talking in the back of the shop. You must have seen them? Zach, did you see them?'

'No Izzie. Come on dreamy head. You've been reading too many fairy stories,' said Zach as he looked up at the town clock again. 'It's nearly ten to four. We need to get going, we're going to be a little late as it is.'

Izzie bent down to give Millie a pat.

'I bet you saw them didn't you girl, eh?' Millie lifted up a single paw.

'I thought so,' said Izzie giving Millie a big smile.

As they were passing the clock tower Izzie suddenly had pictures in her mind of her riding a horse into battle and something about a queen of the waters out in the fen. Finally, for a fleeting second she saw an enormous mountain that began to fade away as she tried desperately to keep it in her head.

'Come on Izzie, you old slowcoach,' urged a smiling Zach.

'Step on it. Get a move on. Fly Canaries fly.'

EPILOGUE

Izzie still sometimes wonders quite what it was that Abi saw when, as a little girl walking across the bridge over the relief channel at Downham Market, she stopped at the one hundred and fortieth rail on the Kings Lynn side and stared down into the waters below. Indeed she can't be sure that Abi saw anything at all. To be truthful, you can never be certain of anything out in the mysterious kingdom of the fen.

However, when young Izzie stands by the one hundred and fortieth rail and sees a beautiful swan swimming gracefully around, occasionally dipping its head below the water to check that everything is in good order in its watery world, she is sure that there is every chance that it is Aquavena.